D0160532

Chaos Theory

Also by Nic Stone

Dear Martin

Odd One Out

Jackpot

Dear Justyce

Chaos Theory

NIC STONE

CROWN

NEW YORK

Text copyright © 2023 by Logolepsy Media Inc.
Jacket art copyright © 2023 by Cienna Smith

All rights reserved. Published in the United States by Crown Books for Young Readers, an imprint of Random House Children's Books, a division of Penguin Random House LLC, New York.

Crown and the colophon are registered trademarks of Penguin Random House LLC.

Visit us on the Web! GetUnderlined.com

Educators and librarians, for a variety of teaching tools, visit us at RHTeachersLibrarians.com

Library of Congress Cataloging-in-Publication Data is available upon request.
ISBN 978-0-593-30770-0 (trade)—ISBN 978-0-593-30771-7 (lib. bdg.)—
ISBN 978-0-593-30772-4 (ebook)

The text of this book is set in 11.15-point Berling LT Std.
Interior design by Jen Valero

Printed in the United States of America
10 9 8 7 6 5 4 3 2 1
First Edition

For my beloved father, Tony A. Bouie.
Thank you for always rooting for me as me.

Dearly beloved reader:

We are gathered here today to . . . read this book about brain-based stuff that affects a lot of people even though we don't like talking about it.

Yes, that was corny, but hopefully you snorted or sucked your teeth or rolled your eyes or something. The ice needed to be broken.

Now that I have your full attention, let me first say this: I loooooathe the term "mental illness." Yes, I know where it comes from and why we use it, but the idea of there being a *right* way for a brain to function is . . . well, I find it endlessly annoying, and as you read this book, I hope you'll see why.

But since you haven't read it yet, I want to tell you up front that I, Nic Stone, am *technically* mentally ill. I won't get into my specific diagnoses here because they're genuinely not important, but I do want to warn you that a lot of what you'll see in these pages is based on my literal personal experiences.

This is an important thing to remember as you read because there's a good chance that (1) if you also live with a brain that functions differently than it's "supposed" to, your experiences will differ from mine, and (2) because of the "mental illness" stigma (which *will* be addressed, thank you very much), there's also a chance you'll have moments where you're like "Omg I *cannot* believe Nic

Stone put this in a book! She's making people with (*insert diagnosis*) look bad!"

But that's the thing: getting rid of the mental illness stigma means getting rid of the idea that what people experience based on their brain chemistry can make them socially unacceptable. Like we all want people to think we're so strong and tough and invincible. But . . . we're not. We're human. For instance: when I'm in the thick of a major depressive episode, my brain tells me I'm trash and I'm worthless and I don't deserve to be alive. Are any of these things true? No. Does *knowing* they're not true make me *feel* them less acutely? Nope. Self-hatred is one of my depressive symptoms, in a similar way that having a runny nose is a symptom of a head cold. In and of itself, it's just a thing that IS.

My point in all this: while there IS an official content warning, know that I'm not going to sugarcoat anything in this book. If you are living with brain chemistry that functions in a way that occasionally obliterates your innate survival instincts, definitely think twice about reading this because there is some triggering content in here.

Which brings me to the strangest thing I'll probably ever say: while this book is written *for* individuals who live with or have experienced any of the varying forms of mental illness, it's written *to* the people who don't really *get* how mental illness "works" and who receive a lot of their information about it from sources that honestly don't *get* it either.

My hope, as with all of my books, is that no matter *how* your brain works, you'll close this story with a greater understanding of the fact that (1) humanity on the whole is quite beautiful even when it defies our expectations, and (2) people need the space—and compassion—to be fully human. Also, our experiences affect us FAR more than we let on.

Anyway, happy reading.

Oh! And spoiler alert: even with my diagnoses, I'm doing just fine. Thriving, actually. As evidenced (for me) by the fact that—VOILA!—I've written another book.

CONTENT WARNING:

The following story contains mentions of self-harm and suicide. If you are struggling with the former or contemplating the latter, know that you are not alone, but also, please read with caution.

April 5.

It's been almost a year, but I still think about you every day and wish I could go back and do things diffenestg.

Differently*

That's super sweet, but I think you have the wrong number.

Oh. Is this 6785552535?

Nope. Look again. You're off a digit.

Oh man . . .

Well maybe its a sign . . .

DO uyou believe in signs, wrong number person?

I'm gonna go now. Sorry
I'm not who you thought I was.

Wait, don't go!

Pleasese

Please*. Sorry. Bub=mble thumbs,

Anyway, I know you don't know me,
but maybe it's better like this.

Umm . . . what's better like what?

I mean, texting you was an accident,
right?

but like . . .

Maybe your who I was
SUPPOSED to text? Because
you don't know me

And I clearkly need somebOdy to talk to.

Maybe the anonymousness is a presngt or something.

Present* Like a gift.

You there?

Heklo?'

Shit. Sorry. I've have too mich tp drink Shoula left my phone in my pocket.

Anonymity.

What?

The noun form of anonymous is anonymity.

Oh.

Yeah I think/ I mayhbe knew that

I get good grased in enhlish classes.

English*

Which Im;m clearly struggling to typa.

TYPE*

Jesus.

Uhhh . . . I'm not really sure what to say?

Never been an anonymous emotional support person before. But you are certainly in need of one.

HA! Well win u put it like that . . .

I hope that wasn't offensive.

Nah, it's ffine.

It's not like you're wrong. That's baskiallhy what I asked for. Anaonymous emotional support person

Without ACTUALLY asking, by the way.

Just thought I'd point that out.

Omdeed!

Indeed.*

Who were you TRYING to reach by the way? If you don't mind my asking . . .

My uhh . . . ex.

Ah.

Yeah.

And I take it things didn't end well?

takes another swim

Swig*

First piece of anonymous, unsolicited advice:

Maybe don't have any more to drink?

Touché anonymousness ananyomity friend

Are you at home by chance?

Nope. Friend's house. Ragering party Snort.

Don't think I've ever seen anyone type out the word "snort" before.

U know what they say: First time for everything.

Thouagh Im never sure who "they" actually are.

Will you do me a favor?

I mean, you're still talking to me

WOud ceetainly say I owe you one.

Certainly*

Don't drive home.

Okay?

You there?

Yeah, I'm here.

Alright. I wonty.

7

You promise?

Hello?

Where'd you go?

Just fin/isned my drink.

Time for another 1.

[anonymous unsoliciyed advice DENIED!]

Okay.

Do you promise you won't drive though?

Okay.

I prom,ose I won'y dribe,

Promise* I won't*

drive.

Thank you.

Glad to hear it.

Okauy

I'm gonna go now.

Thanks for talking to me.

Nl/ghty nite.

PHASE 1

Stellar
Nebula

(Un)remarkable.

Shelbi Augustine is having a weird night. The weirdest since she moved to this weird little not-city (Peachtree Corners) in this weird state (Georgia).

But she can't figure out how to feel about it.

She's in the backseat of the car that carts her everywhere she needs to go, but as Mario—the driver—sits, drumming his fingers on the steering wheel and waiting for the entry gate to her home to yawn open, Shelbi feels like she's in some black-hole-accessed parallel universe. She sighs and looks down at her phone again.

First there was that downright bizarre text exchange. No clue who the guy was—or if it even *was* a guy—but the whole thing shook her down to her carbon-filled core.

Then Part B: on the way home, there was traffic. Car accident. Which . . . wasn't the least bit surprising considering how grotesquely people drive in this funky little suburb. But it *was* annoying—she was ready to be in her bed, curled up and eyes shut, with the artificial sounds of a gently bubbling brook flowing into her ears.

The wreck itself looked fairly straightforward: based on the position of the vehicle, the tire tracks on the road, and the location of the damage to the car, Shelbi presumes the driver was headed eastbound on Spalding Drive just like she and Mario were, but for some reason or another, said driver lost control, experienced a spinout, and threw the passenger side into a tree on the right side of the two-lane road.

Simple and frankly unremarkable.

However, as they crept past the wreck, she could've sworn she saw Andy Criddle sitting in the back of a police cruiser.

Which *was* remarkable. To Shelbi at least.

Not that she's ever spoken to him before. They do have AP Physics together, but she's only been at Windward Academy since the start of the school year. Because she came in as a senior and knew she wouldn't be there very long, she hasn't really bothered speaking to anyone.

It's occurring to her now how not-normal that is. Especially when it comes to Andy Criddle. Because . . . well, Shelbi knows Andy's dad. Like, pretty well. He's this super-dope white dude who runs the soup kitchen at the City Mission where Shelbi volunteers every Saturday morning.

In that space, she's everybody's favorite. When it comes to her peers, though? Well, what Shelbi *is* sure of is that what her classmates don't know can't be used to hurt her like it was at her last school.

And anyway, the closer they get to the house, the more Shelbi thinks there's no way that was Andy Criddle. It couldn't have been. Maybe the person just *looked* like him. *Light-skinned dude with buzzed but impeccably lined hair* isn't exactly a rarity in weirdly colorful Peachtree Corners.

Or maybe he didn't look like Andy at all and she just

really needs to sleep. Certainly wouldn't be her first time seeing something that's nothing like what's actually there.

She looks down at her phone again. Maybe she should've said "Nighty-nite" back. (Though who even says that, let alone types it out? And with a *hyphen*?)

She'd text now but . . . *that* would be weird, right? It's been like two hours and is now almost midnight.

Mario pulls to a stop in front of the house. Then he's coming around to open her door. She's precisely 127 steps from her bed.

Almost there.

She puts the phone on Do Not Disturb, drops it into her bag, and climbs out of the car.

Hopefully her mystery messenger is okay.

Whoever they are.

WASTED.

Andy Criddle, though, is very much *not* okay.

At all.

He's had *far* too much to drink. Again. Which is bad.

And things are about to get worse. Because in no more than a minute, all the crap he consumed at Marcus Page's house will make a grand reappearance on the floor of a cop car.

The cop car he's in. In handcuffs. Which are far more uncomfortable than he would've expected.

He can't open his eyes because the blur of passing trees makes him dizzy. But keeping them closed also sucks because the staticky noise from the two-way radio thing keeps stabbing him in the brain.

He wants another drink. Or three. Or a couple bottles . . . Or three. Bottles.

When the cop yelled out "Point-one-two!" after making him blow in the Breathalyzer thing, all he could think was *Damn . . . a couple more shots would've done the trick.*

A couple more, and Andy would've passed out like he was aiming to. He'd still have a car, and he wouldn't be in the back of a police cruiser in handcuffs.

Headed to jail, he supposes.

Whatever.

He still can't believe somebody had the nerve to say the E-word. He downed the shot that sealed his fate (don't ask him what number . . . lost count after five), and somebody—he thinks it was a girl?—touched his arm and said, "Andy, you should stop. Emma wouldn't want to see you like this."

Emma.

EmmaEmmaEmmaEmmaEmmaEmmaEmma . . .

How did the person even *know* Emma? Clearly they knew *Andy* pretty well to have any sort of idea of what his three-year-old sister would or wouldn't have wanted to see.

He had to get out of there. *Had* to.

Marcus tried to keep him from leaving. Andy was obviously in no position to be behind the wheel. Andy's also pretty sure he promised somebody he wouldn't drive. But he can't remember who.

Oh well.

Marcus clearly failed to stop him—being the reigning state judo champion gives Andy a bit of a persuasive edge in situations like these. He didn't have to hurt his buddy, thankfully.

". . . Mr. Criddle?"

That's Andy!

Wait . . . the officer is talking. And looking at Andy in the rearview. Why does the guy have four eyes? Is this an alien abduction? (Not that he would mind being whisked off to another planet . . .)

Andy shakes his head and looks again.

Two eyes. There are two eyes.

"Did you hear me, son?"

"Huh?"

"I said are you sure you don't want to go to the hospital? I'm sure your mom would prefer you get some medical attention before we process you down at the station."

"No thanks," Andy replies. "Jail is fine."

The car turns left, and Andy falls to the right. He groans, and his stomach burbles in agreement.

"Man, it's really somethin' wrong with kids these days," Andy hears the officer mumble under his breath. "I ain't never heard of somebody *wanting* to go to jail."

Cop's got it all wrong, though. It's not that Andy *wants* to go to jail . . .

It's just his best option.

In jail, he'll have protection from Mom's wrath in the form of heavy iron bars. Because the only thing worse than the Windward Academy salutatorian getting an underage DUI a week and a half before graduation is getting said underage DUI during Congresswoman Cris Criddle's Senate campaign.

The cop looked so stunned when he saw *Andy Criddle* sitting on the curb, Andy thought dude would fall over dead. He *was* glad to see that the officer was Black. And that dude seemed to be more disappointed than angry.

Andy couldn't find his wallet to give the nice officer his license—very likely lost in his very totaled car. But it didn't really matter. The cop didn't need it to identify him—

Uh-oh.

"Oh crap—" and Kool-Aid and Captain Morgan's. And Chex Mix.

And . . . cop car.

"Jesus Christ!" the officer roars.

"You shouldn't take the Lord's name in vain, dude." (Those are the words in Andy's mind, but it sounds more like *youshudentaykuhlornimminvaydoo* as it runs out of his mouth on the tail of a drool drip.) He's headed for the crash—figuratively this time.

His head rolls to the side and the tree blur triggers another round of literal comeuppance.

The cop's voice comes louder this time. "I'm trying to be

on your side here, kid—Lord knows I been where you are—
but I swear if you puke in my cruiser one more time—"

"No worries, my man," Andy mumbles as his eyelids
shut. His forehead lands on the window, and he can finally
feel the pull of unconsciousness on his limbs.

Thank God.

Awkward.

It takes every ounce of courage she can muster for Shelbi
to approach Andy Criddle after calc that following Monday. For one, while she knows it's the right thing to do,
returning Andy's wallet will involve telling him how she
got it. And *that's* destined to be awkward.

And then there's the *for two*: as she made her way to
the AP Physics classroom, she happened to be approaching the teachers' lounge next door at the exact moment a
female voice said, ". . . you will be able to keep your title
as salutatorian, but you will *not* be permitted to speak at
commencement."

Shelbi stopped dead. Like, on instinct.

After a male voice responded: "Huh?" the female voice
went on: "Your mother would like to prevent this prohi-
bition from becoming public knowledge, so we've agreed
that I will not release this information provided that you
are not in attendance at the ceremony."

"Hold up. Are you saying I've gone from not being able to *speak* to not being able to *come?*"

"I'm glad we understand each other," the woman replied. And as she exited the small room, she and Shelbi met eyes. It was the Windward Academy headmaster. A tiny blond woman who always conjured the word *barracuda* in Shelbi's mind. Small but mighty, the little lady was absolutely terrifying.

Shelbi dropped her gaze to the impossibly shiny floor.

And just in time, too. Because not a half second later, Andy Criddle stepped into the hallway and made a beeline for the room Shelbi was headed to.

She hoped he didn't notice her.

Safe to say everybody notices *him*, though. Throughout the fifty-five-minute class, it's almost impossible for Shelbi to focus on *relativity*, because all she can think about is how four years of what had to be hard work—*salutatorian* is kind of a big deal, is it not?—were basically nullified by one crap decision. Doesn't help that despite keeping her eyes fixed to the SMART Board, she can see her classmates sneaking glances in Andy's direction from her seat at the back of the room.

Not that she can blame them: from what Shelbi knows about Andy Criddle, he seems to be the prototypical golden boy. SAT Verbal 800 Club, headed to Brown (according to the "Who's Who Among Windward Academy Seniors" web page), and some kind of martial arts state champion to boot. She wouldn't say he's "popular" in the stereotypical sense, but he seems super nice and people definitely like him. He's not too hard on the eyes, either.

And while Shelbi certainly knows from experience that "Academically High-Achieving" and "Occasionally Susceptible to Poor Decision-Making" aren't mutually exclusive, she really *was* surprised to see UNDERAGED SON OF SENATE CANDIDATE DRIVES DRUNK on the front page of Daddy's Sunday paper. With a picture of Andy yacking on a reporter's shoes outside the police station.

By some miracle, the bell rings. Andy doesn't budge from his seat. If he's anything like *her,* he'll let the room empty before even getting out of his seat. Just to avoid the heat of judgmental stares against his back.

Shelbi exits with the others and takes up a post right beyond the doorway.

Then she waits.

And waits.

They only have six minutes between bells, and she's starting to worry. Because two of them have elapsed.

Of course, the moment she turns to look back into the classroom—make sure he's at least gotten out of the chair—he comes barreling through the door. Smacks right into her.

"Whoa!" she says, stumbling back. She knew he was tall, but he's significantly more *solid* than she realized.

"Aww man, I'm sorry," he says. "Are you okay?"

She pulls it together and dusts herself off. "You're excused," she replies, trying to *break the ice*, as they say.

He looks . . . like that's not the response he was expecting.

It makes Shelbi smile. And relax a bit. "I'm just kidding. Kinda my own fault for waiting here all creeperishly," she says. "I just wanted to give you this." And she holds up Andy's wallet. Which, based on the way his eyes widen, he both recognizes and is shocked to see.

Now Shelbi's laughing. And looking him over a bit more closely. He's *really* cute. Far cuter than she realized. ("You know, you really should give light-skinned boys a chance," she can hear her favorite—dark-skinned—cousin saying in her head.)

Shelbi pushes her glasses up on her nose. "I found that in the grass near the tree you hit," she says.

"You . . . Wait, what?"

Right. Because some random girl popping up with your wallet after you total your car is probably a *smidge* discombobulating. "I, uhh . . ." Her chin drops. "Okay, you'll likely think this is super weird, but I like figuring out the physics of car crashes." She looks up to gauge his reaction, but his face is blank. "I happened to pass your accident on Saturday night, so I went back to explore the scene yesterday."

"Oh," he says. "Umm . . . That's an interesting hobby." Translation: he thinks it's super weird. He does, however, take the wallet from her hand. "I appreciate this, though."

Shelbi nods. Relieved. "You're welcome. However, you should know that I know your secret."

"My secret?"

Crap, why did she say THAT?

Now she can't look him in the eye. First time she's having an actual conversation with someone in this stuffy school, and *this* is how it's going.

Classic.

"Yes, umm . . . Well, I sorta had to *open* the wallet to see who it belonged to? And I saw your license. So . . ."

He doesn't say anything, so she lifts her eyes back to his face. He looks terrified. Almost makes her laugh again.

Shelbi knew how *nice* Andy Criddle seemed, but experiencing his complete lack of pretense is so refreshing, she hardly knows what to do with herself. He seems so . . . safe.

She grabs his arm and tugs him down to her level so she can whisper into his ear. "I'm talking about the fact that your first name is *Walter*?" She lets go. "Unless that's not actually a secret . . ."

As he stretches back to his full height, *he* smiles. "Oh. That."

"Yep." She looks at her watch. The smile was kind of a lot and she wasn't ready. "We should get moving. Bell's in one minute and twenty-six seconds."

"True," Andy replies.

But he doesn't budge.

Shelbi doesn't either. They just . . . stare at each other.

And then Shelbi's lips are parting again. "Look, you

have to ignore everyone, okay?" she says, peeking past him to make sure no one else is listening. "When people are giving you dirty looks and stuff? Just remember they're basing their judgments on limited information. You're the only person who *really* knows what you're going through, and *you* may not even be sure, you know? I've totally been there."

"You have?" He draws back, clearly surprised.

Which feels pretty good. Maybe Mama was right about that whole clean slate thing.

"Sure have." She looks at her watch again. "K, we're down to thirty seconds. I'll see you around, yeah?"

He smiles again. *Definitely* a lot.

"Yeah. Okay," he says. "Hey, thanks again." He lifts the wallet.

"Glad to have been of service!" Shelbi says (and regrets it instantly). "Umm . . . bye!"

"Bye . . . hey—"

But Shelbi has no idea what he was going to say because the bell rings.

She turns and rushes away.

Hey.

You uh . . . you there?

Hey.

I am. Here.

Whew, thank God

Admittedly surprised to hear from you again . . .

You did mean to text ME and not the ex-girlfriend this time, right?

Yes. Definitely YOU.

Whoever you are.

I'm sober this time. And totally lucid.

24

Ah. Congratulations!

So what can I do for you?

More anonymous emotional support?

Umm . . . yes. If that's okay with you?

Shoot.

Well something happened today and I dunno . . .

As strange (and probably creepy) as it sounds, you're the only person I think I can tell about it without feeling like a crazy person.

A crazy person, huh?

Do tell.

Well, I kinda wrecked my car on Saturday night.

Wait.

Come again?

Yeah. I uhhh . . . might've broken my promise to you. Which I'm really sorry about.

Anyway, today at school, a girl I've never spoken to before brought me my wallet.

You still there?

Hello?

Sorry.

Why would a girl you've never spoken to before have your wallet?

She said she found it near the scene of the accident.

That's interesting . . .

Right?

She said she likes to figure out car crash physics or something.

Which I thought was kinda weird at first . . . But then the more I thought about it, it's oddly . . . cute?

Cute.

Yeah. SHE is also pretty cute.

She wears these cat-eye glasses that she cutely pushes up on her nose . . .

And she's got these dimples when she smiles. Man.

Well that's good to hear . . .

If you're gonna be a weirdo, at least be a cute one?

That's one way to look at it I guess.

The thing I can't stop thinking about is how . . . OK she made me feel.

Well that's good.

Yeah. It's like I was MEANT to talk to exactly her at that particular moment in time.

It's the same way I felt when I was talking to you about Steph.

Steph?

My ex.

Ah. Right.

28

Okay.

So does this mystery girl have a name?

Well, that's the embarrassing thing . . .

I don't know it.

You don't know it??

She was new this year!

And you didn't ask??

I mean, I didn't want her to KNOW
I didn't know it . . .

So what you're saying is you're basically
the worst?

Hey, don't judge me. I've had a lot on my
mind.

Yeah okay. I'll give you that.

Wait . . . how old are you?

Just turned eighteen.

I really want to talk to her again.

So do.

But I don't know anything about her.

You . . . also don't know anything about me?

Yeah, but that's the point of anonymity, isn't it?

Like what the hell would I even say to her?

Well, I mean . . .

How bout you start by asking her name?

Touché anonymous emotional support pal.

Touché.

MISSION.

Except Andy doesn't.

Ask her name.

In fact, despite having *two* classes together, they don't exchange a single word for the rest of the week.

And it's not just on him. He *swears* it's not. While, yes, he totally punked out on Tuesday—partially because he was hungover; Monday night had been a doozie—on Wednesday, he was almost about to say something. There was this moment when they met eyes just before passing each other in the hallway, and he totally opened his mouth . . . but she quickly looked away and sped up.

He spent the rest of the day wondering if there was something on his face.

Thursday was a blur because he was still a little drunk from the night before. And Friday just sucked: Andy's mom's lawyer—well, *Andy's* lawyer now—stopped by to deliver the news that in addition to the loss of his license for six months (God), "The judge is gonna slap you with forty hours of mandatory community service when you go before him next month." Told him he *might as well get a jump on it.*

Which is why at 7:45 a.m. on Saturday, Andy Criddle, king of the weekend sleep-in, is beside Dad in his pickup truck, being subjected to Kenny Chesney's warbly sung sadness, en route to the City Mission.

And . . . he's hungover.

As they pull into the parking lot, Andy spots a massive Mercedes-Benz idling at the curb near the entrance to the building. He and Dad exit the pickup at the same moment the Benz driver—as in *chauffeur:* full suit, goofy cap, the whole shebang—steps out to open the back door.

Andy's expecting some big-deal Donor-for-the-Tax-Deduction to climb out. So when precisely whom he *wouldn't* expect—the wallet-returning girl from his class whose name he doesn't know because he still hasn't asked her—climbs out instead, Andy freezes, wide-eyed, like he's just sighted Black Santa.

"You all right over there, son?" Dad says.

"Uhhh . . ."

She looks different, though Andy can't seem to pinpoint why. Her hair is in a thick braid that drapes over her shoulder, and she's wearing a long (and fitted) black skirt with a super-nerdy (and fitted) math T-shirt ($\sqrt{-1}$ 2^3 Σ π, AND IT WAS DELICIOUS!). There's a gentle yet distinctive sway to her hips, and after Andy takes her in as a whole, he puts his eyes on her face and tries (struggles) to keep them there.

She waves and pushes her cat-eye glasses up on the bridge of her nose. And that's when it hits him: she's not in her school uniform. It also occurs to him that he's staring pretty hard. So instead of waving back like a normal person, he looks down at his shoes.

Which is when he hears, "Hey, Shels!" in Dad's voice.

Andy's head pops up.

"Hi, Charlie!" she replies as she gives Dad a hug.

Wait. "You two know each other?" Andy asks.

"We sure do," Dad says. "Shelbi's been volunteering here every Saturday for, what? The past six months, Shels?"

So her name is Shelbi. (*Why is it bugging Andy that Dad keeps calling her Shels?*)

"Something like that," she—*Shelbi*—says, and then she reaches out to hug Andy. Which he's not expecting, so it's awkward. "Fancy seeing you here, Walter . . ."

Dad gives Andy a look like *Walter?* And Andy shrugs. So Dad shrugs too.

"How's my favorite future Ramblin' Wreck on this lovely Saturday morning?" Dad then asks.

"I'm great!" And she smiles (man, those *dimples*). "Thanks for asking."

Andy—or is he *Walter* now?—clears his throat as a second piece of the cute-physics-nerd-girl puzzle slides into place. "So, you're headed to Georgia Tech, huh?"

"That I am."

Andy-Walter doesn't think he's ever seen anyone look prouder.

"Astrophysics, right?" Dad nudges her with an elbow.

She chuckles. "That's the plan. And you're Brown-bound, yeah, Walter?"

"Yep," Andy (Walter) says, a little puffed up by the fact that she knows. "Poli sci."

"Can you tell which parent is his favorite? Kid picked his mom's alma mater *and* her major."

34

Andy laughs. It's a legitimate sore spot for the old man. Dad is an industrial engineer and always hoped his only son would be a tennis star at Georgia Tech like he was.

Andy has disappointed on all counts. "I'm sure my dad's ready to adopt you since you're going to *his* school," he says to Shelbi.

"You better believe I am." Dad throws an arm around her shoulders and gives her a squeeze, and a little bloom of jealousy shoots up and out of Andy's chest like a noxious gas cloud.

He glances over at Dad. In his Levi's and his tucked plaid shirt with the sleeves rolled back over his muscly forearms, the guy looks like a swaggy lumberjack. Like dude from that one paper towel brand, *Brawny* (and how fitting is the name?). Never in a million years would Andy have thought he'd be competing with his freaking *dad* for a girl's affections.

Of course, all of this is completely irrational, but there's no reasoning with the gale-force fury of masculine jealousy. Andy can feel the heat in his cheeks, so he looks away and takes a deep breath.

He makes a decision right then and there: If this *Shelbi* doesn't leave the Mission today at least as comfortable with Andy as she is with Mr. Tall, Tan & Handsome over there (the jerk), Andy's exiling himself to a monastery in the mountains. Because he'll obviously never succeed with women.

Service.

Shelbi's gonna have to tell him. She knows this much.

She's just not exactly sure *how*.

"So, you're really here every Saturday?" Walter asks her as she plops a scoop of scrambled eggs on the plate of a man named Steven.

"She sure is, and so am I, just to see her," Steven replies with a wink.

It makes Shelbi laugh.

Steven goes on: "Be smart, young man. Don't let a gal like that get away from ya, hear?"

"Yes, sir," from Walter. (It's *so* weird that he's here. Like . . . beside her. He smells kinda good, too . . .)

But how would Shelbi even bring it up? *Oh, by the way: That mystery person you've been text-baring your soul to? Yeah, it's totally me. And I also think* you're *cute*—

"He seems interesting," Walter says. Shelbi knows he's been trying to get her talking since they put their hairnets on.

"Oh, he certainly is," she replies. And she exhales. This is something she *can* talk about. She's gotten so close to some of these people, she knows their individual stories by heart. "Steven graduated from Georgia Tech in the 1990s and was a successful engineer. But then he got mixed up in some shady stuff during that economic crash when we were like three, and he wound up losing his job, his home, his family . . . everything. He was totally clean for about six months until he relapsed a few weeks ago."

"Wow. Any idea what . . . caused it? The relapse, I mean."

"I haven't verified this with him, but word is he found out his dad passed away. And Steve hadn't spoken to him in years."

Walter nods, and a look Shelbi can't decipher passes over his face. "Grief will certainly do that to a person. Poor guy."

"Yeah." Not knowing what to make of his response, Shelbi points to someone else. A white lady with stringy hair and a far-off look in her eyes. "See her? That's Angela." (Shelbi could do this all day.) "I met her about a month ago and convinced her to start coming here for food. I'd gone to the gas station across the street, and she approached me to ask if I had any maxi-pads."

Walter doesn't respond. Not that Shelbi was expecting him to. It's part of the reason she picked the woman.

"The whole thing really shook me," Shelbi goes on. "You're a guy so it probably doesn't make sense to you, but her needing *maxi-pads* was a jarring reminder that the people who come here haven't ceased to be human, you know?"

She's able to keep it up—the sharing of people stories—for a few minutes more, but then things shift to a discussion about whether or not some of the things people in the room have done qualify as unforgivable mistakes. And Walter is far more open and thoughtful than Shelbi expects him to be—though she's not sure why her expectations of him were so low. Bottom line, she enjoys the conversation immensely. To the point that when it's time for her to go home, she's genuinely sad about it ending.

She also knows she *has* to tell him *she's* his anonymous emotional support pal. Her brain might ooze out of her ears if she doesn't.

When she pops into the kitchen to hang her apron, Charlie smiles at her.

"My knucklehead son didn't cause you too much trouble, did he?"

Shelbi laughs. "Ah, he's a good egg."

"I think he might like you. Certainly doesn't listen that intently when *I'm* talk—"

"Daaaaaad."

Charlie laughs. "How long you been eavesdropping, ya creep?" he asks as that *knucklehead son* comes fully into the room.

Walter just glares at him. "I'll walk you out," he says to Shelbi.

They head to the exit in silence, but the moment they're outside, she opens her mouth to speak. "So I need to tell—"

"You're *really* here every Saturday?" he says at the same time. "Oh. My bad. Didn't mean to cut you off."

"No problem," Shelbi says. "And yes: I really am here every Saturday."

"Huh. That's kind of amazing."

"Let's sit," Shelbi says, dropping down onto the curb. Walter follows suit.

There's a beat of awkward silence. Then she opens her mouth to try again—

"Thanks again for bringing me my wallet." (It would seem that Walter Andrew Criddle is just as uncomfortable with conversational lulls as Shelbi is.)

"You're welcome," she replies. "Again."

"I . . . umm . . . I also appreciate what you said. Probably sounds strange, but it was exactly what I needed to hear."

Okay. It's time.

"I need to tell you something," Shelbi begins. Totally shifts the air and she kinda hates it.

"Okay . . . ," he replies.

"Remember how the night of your accident, you were talking to someone?"

"Mmmm . . . I talked to a lot of people that night."

"This was over text."

He doesn't respond. Shelbi peeks over at him. He's just gazing out across the parking lot.

"Umm . . . did you hear me?"

"Are you about to tell me it's been you the whole time?"

"Yes."

Again: silence.

"For what it's worth, I had no idea you were *you* until Monday. When you were talking to me about . . . me," Shelbi says.

"Well, this is embarrassing."

They both go quiet, but now Shelbi's pulse is speeding up. She needs to say something else.

"I forgive you, you know" is what comes out.

"Huh?"

"For breaking your promise." Now she looks at him. "I've gotten one before too."

Andy looks at her, clearly *not* following.

"A DUI?" She bumps him with her shoulder. "Actually, mine was not a DUI but an MIP—that's minor in possession of alcohol—"

"Oh, I'm aware," Walter says, fully tuned in now.

"Yeah, well, I also got hit with fake ID violation *and* driving without a license." *Why is she telling him all this?*

"Well, damn," he says.

At that, Mario pulls up, and Walter stands to open Shelbi's door. "So, you literally have a whole chauffeur?" he says as she climbs in.

"Yeah, don't remind me. No offense, Mario." She pats Mario on the shoulder, and he nods. "For what it's worth, I got my license two weeks ago. But between the two of us, I'm not real confident about the way you *Georgia* drivers do things."

Walter laughs.

It smacks Shelbi then: she *really* likes making him laugh. And like . . . chatting. "You know, you're way too easy to talk to," she says.

He snorts. "You're probably the only person on earth who feels that way," he replies, shifting his gaze to some far-off point Shelbi knows is out of her reach.

"Ummm . . ." *Is she really about to do this?* "So I know we technically just met or whatever. But you *do* have my number. I know we're not anonymous anymore, but I'm around if you need to talk."

And she instantly wants to suck the words back into her mouth and swallow them down. Because she doesn't *do* peer relationships anymore after what happened. So why would she say that? And *mean* it?

"Wow, umm . . ." Walter's cheeks go all rosy, and Shelbi hates the flip it causes in her stomach. Why does he have to be so cute? It's annoying. "That's . . . really nice of you," he says.

Shelbi shrugs. "I'll bill ya later." And she winks. (What is she *doing?*)

Walter smiles. Big. And bright.

Shelbi smiles back. "I'll see you around, yeah?"

"Yeah. Okay."

She starts to pull the door shut, but he stops it. "Hey," he says. And he holds up his phone. "Thank you."

"What on earth are you thanking me for this time, Walter?"

He thinks on it for a second, then looks Shelbi right in the eye. "For judgment-free safety," he says. And then he closes the car door.

41

CHICKEN.

The grief always hits Andy the hardest at dusk. Like right before the horizon swallows the sun. That had been the last thing he saw before he drifted off to sleep on the day that changed his life irrevocably.

The scream that woke him up will likely ring through his skull forever.

Now, though, Andy's staring out his bedroom window at the sinking ball of fire that keeps the earth at the perfect temperature to sustain life. He takes another swig from his judo water bottle. Which does not contain water. Dad did a thorough sweep of Andy's room after his arrest and collected every bottle of liquor he could find . . . but he didn't find all of them.

Andy really wants to call Shelbi. But a drunk dial maybe wouldn't be a good look now that she knows who he is.

He could text but . . . what would he even say? *Nice chatting with you today* feels corny. *You looked killer out of uniform*, though true, feels a bit strong.

Yeah, never mind. It's not like she could do very much for him right now anyway.

He screws the top onto his bottle. The cheap bourbon inside it is pretty disgusting.

Dulls the ache, though.

Definitely in for the night. Hopefully Dad doesn't decide to come "check on" Andy (or is he Walter now?).

Walter-Andy's vision is beginning to blur, but still: he watches as the top edge of the sun disappears.

Walter?

Are you busy?

You know what's weird?

What?

Being called Walter.

I mean, I can stop if you want . . .

Nah, you don't have to. I just gotta
get used to it.

It can be out setret thing.

our* secret* thing.

Our secret thing, huh?

Yup.

Well okay then . . .

Are you okay?

Chillin like a villain. All good in the hooood.

Ah

How much have you had to drink this evening?

What makes you think I hasd omething ti drubk?

Wow, trying that again:

What makes you think* I* had* something* to* drink*?

Look, I know I have a baby face with the dimples and all. But I wasn't born yesterday.

45

That's actually good.

This whole thing would be weird is you were.

If

Right . . .

Umm . . . Anyway.

I was just texting to see what you thought of the City Mission today since we didn't really get to talk about it.

But maybe this isn't the best time?

I

loved every minute of it.

But that's probably because you were there.

Well alright then.

Sorry if that was too atsrong. Just mean you feel nice to be around.

strong*

Oh.

That's kind of you to say.

I speak only truth.

Lol, you're totally going to regret being this open when you read through these tomorrow.

Likely.

But at least you'll know the real truth if I start avioding you again.

Not real big on letting people in huh?

Don't know that I would've ever thought to put it like that.

But yeah.

Definitely not the "open book" type.

Well look at that.

We have things in common besides making poor decisions while intoxicated.

Huh?

What do you mean?

I'm not much of an open book either.

You at home?

And planning to stay there?

Yeah.

Glad to hear it.

Do me (and you) a favor?

Yeah.

Pop a couple ibuprofen and drink some water.

Oh absoluetly.

You're gonna be feeling this tomorrow.

Yup.

Gifted.

Shelbi looks over at her phone.

It's been across the room on her desk, facedown, since she sent that last message to Walter-Andy two hours ago.

She sighs and puts her book down. It's not like she's absorbed anything she's read since grabbing something random off the shelf and curling up in bed. Her mind has been elsewhere. Else . . . *whom*? Is that a thing? She's being ridiculous about this and she knows it, but she also knows there's a lot she *doesn't* know. Especially about *him*.

He just seems so . . . sad. Which is something Shelbi can definitely relate to, considering her diagnoses. But how do you tell somebody that? *Hey, so as a person living with a bona fide mood disorder who deals with high levels of existential sadness, I can tell you're pretty down. Wanna talk about it?* feels a bit on the nose.

She did totally tell him about that string of charges she landed back in Cali when things were super bad, but she didn't mention any of the brain stuff attached to it. Which . . . would that have been helpful? Considering the frequency with which he seems to drink, Shelbi would say he's got brain stuff going on too.

She sits up and swings her legs over the edge of the bed. Stares across the room. On the desk beside the phone is a set of keys. Which is the thing she'd *actually* wanted to talk about when she reached out to Walter-Andy. She just couldn't figure out how to bring it up once he responded with the whole *It's weird being called Walter* thing. Interacting with peers can be so complicated.

Anyway, what she wanted to tell him was that she'd gotten a "gift" this afternoon and couldn't figure out how she felt about it. She wrote about the whole thing in her journal, but . . . it didn't ease her mind the way it usually would've. It would appear that talking to Walter this afternoon and actually receiving feedback shifted something inside her. Which feels as monumental as Neptune and Pluto swapping places every 248 years and literally changing the solar system.

Shelbi looks back and forth between the phone and the keys. She still can't even believe the keys exist. The whole ordeal had been so bizarre, starting with Mama busting in on Shelbi's afternoon yoga session, looking like she'd debunked the mystery of dark matter. Shelbi hadn't seen the woman that excited since *Cookies and Cream*, a novel she (Mama) wrote, hit #1 on the bestseller list.

"Come, come, come, come!" she said. Just *beaming*. It should've been evident in that very moment that whatever Mama had up her sleeve would rock Shelbi to her core. She practically drug Shelbi down the stairs and out the front door.

When Shelbi saw what was sitting in the driveway— with a giant bow on the roof—her neurons went haywire. Like she literally felt a little *zap* in her brain like in that

Operation game where you have to remove organs and stuff from a naked white dude's body without touching the sides of the holes. (Whose idea was it to make a game like that?)

Daddy could definitely tell something was wrong. He shot Mama his signature *Uh-oh, she's about to crack* look, and then they approached Shelbi slowly, speaking in their "calming voices" about how it's time for Shelbi to "become more autonomous" since she's headed to college in just a few months. Daddy then took Shelbi's hand and led her over to the (brand-new) "gift" while Mama followed on Shelbi's heels, yakking away. ("This car got really high safety ratings, sweetheart!")

All Shelbi remembers after that is Daddy asking her to drive him to the store. And when they got back, he and Mama told Shelbi that Mario would continue driving her to school, but Shelbi would have to drive herself everywhere else she needed to go: therapies, psychiatry appointments, the City Mission, the assisted-living facility where she volunteers a couple times per week, the places she goes hiking . . .

And it's not that Shelbi has a *problem* with driving and getting more independent—that's why she got a driver's license. It's more that she's not sure how to feel about the *type* of car she'll be cruising around in.

Which is why she's annoyed in addition to being grateful. Her parents *know* how she feels about the whole conspicuous consumption thing. They're the ones who sent her abroad so she could "see how good" she has it. And after watching Walter (Andy) interact with *his* dad, Shelbi was pretty sure she could talk to her no-longer-anonymous text buddy about parent stuff.

She shakes her head and falls back onto her bed. Largely to keep from going to grab her phone.

Andy/Walter's at home drunk (again) and certainly in no position to listen to her be all panicky about a thing many people would give their right arm for—which is super problematic, but she won't get into that right now.

She hopes that he's okay. And that he sobers up. Because despite her reservations, she still really wants to talk to him.

RIDE.

At three-thirty the following afternoon, Andy is perched on his porch steps awaiting the arrival of the big black Benz. Was he shocked when he received a Shelbi text at nine a.m. that said

> Hey, I'm going to this play at the Fox tonight, but my cousin just bailed on me. Interested in coming with?

Absolutely.

But even more shocking to him is how quickly he said yes.

At 3:34, an Audi A4 Andy can only describe as *obsidian* in color turns the corner and creeps down his street. When it slows to a stop in front of his house, Andy's stomach jumps up into his throat. He's seen one too many gangster movies where a really nice car with darkly tinted windows crawls down a street and then eases to a stop as the back window rolls down and someone starts shooting.

The car does stop. And park. And Andy is totally holding his breath when Shelbi Augustine's head pops up over the roof from the driver's side. "You coming?" she yells.

Fighting to keep the astonishment off his face, Andy stands and unnecessarily dusts his shorts off before heading across the lawn, opening the passenger door, and sliding in. Because that's what you do in a car like this one: you *slide* in.

"Seat belt," she says, once she's back inside and buckling her own. Then she pulls off at the same dreadfully slow pace as before.

There are a few seconds of awkward silence. Then Andy clears his throat. Because he has to ask. "So . . . this *your* car?"

"Yep," she says.

"Is it . . . uhh . . . new?" (Because it definitely *smells* new.)

Her jaw tightens this time, but Andy pretends not to notice. "Mmhmm," she says.

"Wow." Andy runs a fingertip over the wood paneling

in the door and looks around. The word that pops into his head is *opulent*. "It's pretty sick, Shelbi."

When she doesn't reply, he shifts his focus to her. Andy doesn't think he's ever seen anyone grip a steering wheel that tight. "Are you okay?"

She sighs. "I just . . . Can we not talk about it?"

"What?"

"The car."

"Oh." Interesting . . . "Okay."

"Sorry. I know it's weird."

Andy doesn't respond. Because it *is* weird. But he can't exactly say that, can he?

She goes on. "I just can't yet. Eventually."

"All right," Andy replies.

"For now, a change of subject is in both of our best interests."

"Okay." (Why are girls so . . . enigmatic?) "What's your middle name?" Andy asks.

Shelbi smiles, and the dimples appear. The tension disperses, and Andy knows he picked a most excellent change of subject. "Camille. Why?"

Andy shrugs. "You know mine, so I figured it's only fair."

He relaxes into the supple leather as they (finally) reach the entrance to his neighborhood—a journey that takes *him* all of forty-five seconds but has taken Shelbi a good three minutes. She's taking the fifteen-miles-per-hour speed limit signs very seriously. (*Despite the fact that we're in a brand-new Audi A4 that can do at least 130 miles per hour,* Andy thinks but doesn't say.)

Shelbi looks left, right, left again, right again, left again—there's not another car in sight, by the way—before finally pulling out onto the main road. She is by far the most cautious teenage driver Andy has ever encountered.

"Sorry I was late," she says. "Took me longer to get to you than I was expecting. Did you know we're basically neighbors?"

"We are?"

"Yeah, but only on foot. There's a field behind your house, right?"

"Yep."

"My house is on the other side of it."

Andy's glad Shelbi's eyes are on the road. He's *sure* he looks like she just told him she moonlights as the tooth fairy. On the other side of the field behind Andy's house is a mansion the color of cotton candy. Andy can see its extravagant back façade and huge in-ground pool from his house's guest room window.

Until he saw it being painted last year, it was empty for as long as he can remember. "The pink . . . house?"

"That's the one. Hideous, isn't it?" Shelbi says. "Why my mom had it painted the color of watered-down Pepto-Bismol is beyond me."

Andy wants to laugh—it's not an inaccurate description. But . . . he can't. "So, um—"

"You want to know what my parents do for a living, right?" Shelbi offers.

Andy doesn't reply (the answer is yes), but it turns out he doesn't have to.

"My dad's a neurosurgeon, and my mom's a . . . writer."

"A writer?"

"Yes."

"Why'd you hesitate?"

"Because I didn't want you to ask what she writes."

Andy laughs. It feels good. "Well, now you have to tell me."

Shelbi glances over at him and sighs. She really is ridiculously cute. "No judgment?" she says.

"Cross my heart." *Could it really be that bad?*

"My mom writes Urban Romance novels. Four have been made into movies that were pretty solid blockbusters, and the fifth is in production."

"Dang."

"Yep. Her pen name is Shonda Crenshaw."

Andy's . . . not sure he heard her correctly. "Shonda Chenshaw?" he asks.

"That's her."

"You mean Shonda Crenshaw, author of *Thug Love* Shonda Crenshaw?"

Her eyebrows lift, though she doesn't take her eyes off the road. "Walter Criddle knows *Thug Love?*"

"Marcus—You know Marcus Page, right?"

Shelbi snorts. "Is there anybody at our school who *doesn't* know Marcus Page?"

"Touché. Well, I saw *Thug Love* with him. It was . . . vivid."

Shelbi laughs. Despite knowing how cliché it is, Andy's beginning to equate her laughter with music. "I didn't realize you two were friends," she says. "You seem very different."

"You mean how I have the second-highest GPA in our class, whereas he'd be voted 'Most Likely to Impregnate the Entire Cheerleading Team'?"

She laughs again. "That's one way to put it."

"We've been in the same Scout troop since we were Cubs."

They pull to a stop at a red light, and she turns to him. "You're totally an Eagle, aren't you?"

Why is Andy's face so hot? "I am."

"I knew it. Well, don't tell, but I totally have a huge crush on Marcus."

Andy instantly feels like there's a roaring lion inside his abdomen. He couldn't form a response if someone paid him to.

"It's completely insubstantial, and I have no desire to date him," Shelbi continues. "I just think we'd make cute babies."

Again: girls. are. enigmatic. as. hell.

"Well, for what it's worth . . ." (Andy can't believe he's about to say this, but he is.) "I love Marcus like a brother, but he's a moron. Not to break your heart, but the guy is *fully* convinced he's gonna marry Rihanna."

She laughs again, and Andy feels better because she's laughing at something *he* said.

In your face, Marcus Page.

Crisis.

The ride back is . . . tense. Shelbi can only guess that this was Walter's first time seeing *RENT* because from the moment the final curtain closed, he's looked like he witnessed an exorcism.

He doesn't say a word for the entire drive.

Shelbi pulls into the Criddle driveway this time. And once the car is in park, though she's nervous about it (she's really not trying to be all up in his business), she turns to him. "So I'm not sure what's going on in that brain of yours, and I don't want to overstep. But you do have my number. Please don't hesitate to use it if you need to."

Walter looks her in the eye then. And to Shelbi's utter surprise, he says, "Would you mind sitting with me for a bit?"

Shelbi smiles—even though it feels slightly inappropriate to? "It'd be my pleasure."

They exit the car and head up the walkway, then sit on the top porch step. It's exactly where he was sitting when she arrived, so there's almost this feeling of coming full circle. Well, to Shelbi at least.

For a few minutes, they both just stare out across the lawn at the dusky sky. It reminds Shelbi that in about five hours, when the sky is ocean-deep dark, Venus, Mars, Saturn, and Jupiter will be visible behind them in the east. She opens her mouth to crack the tension with this positively exhilarating fact (well, to her at least), but then she hears Walter take a deep breath beside her. He says: "Tom and Angel were really in love, huh?"

That's certainly not what Shelbi was expecting. "Yeah," she says, smiling at the thought of her favorite queer Broadway couple. "They were."

After another short stretch of silence, where it's clear he's not going to say more, Shelbi speaks again: "Guessing you'd never seen *RENT* before?"

"Never heard of it before today."

"Wait, *really?*"

Now Walter smiles. It eases some of the tension in Shelbi's shoulders. "Yep. Not really a musical theater kinda guy."

"Okay. I *guess* that makes sense. So what'd ya think?"

"I . . ." And he stops. Then he turns to her. "Do you believe in God, Shelbi?"

At this, Shelbi laughs. She can't help it. "You're really in crisis right now, huh?"

He puts his head in his hands. "Oh man, you have no idea."

"Wanna talk about it?"

"You see that over there?" He points across the street. There's a CRIDDLE FOR SENATE sign in a neighbor's yard.

"Ah. Well, welcome to the 'My Mom Is Famous' club, I guess?"

Walter snorts. "Mine is more like *infamous*. Cris Criddle is known for five things: her love of the 'Holy Word,' her commitment to corporate capitalism, her zeal for the unborn, her gun collection, and the fact that she's a Black woman holding these views," he says. "And nobody even knows about her disapproval of relationships between people with the same . . . equipment. She keeps that one under wraps."

Shelbi nods. She'd heard all this about the congresswoman—Shelbi's dad certainly isn't Walter's mom's biggest fan (not that she would tell Walter that). But Shelbi's realizing now that she didn't really *believe* any of it. "Is all the stuff she's 'known for' actually true?"

"I honestly have no idea, Shelbi. She's been different since . . . spring break."

"Spring break?"

"Yeah." But he doesn't continue. Just stares at that sign. Shelbi's tempted to go knock it down, but figures maybe that wouldn't be a good idea considering Lady Criddle could be watching from the kitchen window or something.

"Wanna know why I'm weird about the car?" she says instead, hardly believing the words are coming out of her mouth. The only people she's ever told what she's about to share are her parents, grandma, and therapist.

"Do tell," Walter replies.

(Man, Shelbi really hopes she doesn't regret this.) "So.

The summer before my freshman year, my bibi took me on a trip to India—"

"Wait, what's a bibi?"

"Sorry. Bibi is my dad's mom. She's Indian, hence the trip to India."

"Ah," he says. "Okay. Go on."

"The whole visit was really jarring because I'd never seen *real* poverty before," Shelbi continues. "We spent the first week in Bengaluru, and the fact that I could see the slums from the window of our cushy hotel room really messed with my head. Like out one window were all these shiny buildings and shopping malls and nice cars. But out the other, rows and rows of shanties with rusted roofs. And I knew they were filled with people who didn't have enough to eat."

"Wow," Walter says. "That's . . . yeah, I can't even imagine."

"We went to the Taj Mahal toward the end of the trip, but after seeing so much poverty, all I could think about was the fact that the most-visited place in the entire country is literally a giant palace of death," she says. "When we got back to my parents' multimillion-dollar mansion in Los Angeles after flying first class and being chauffeured by our family's personal driver in a two-hundred-thousand-dollar Mercedes, I was literally sick to my stomach. That was my first crisis of faith. I thought if God—who I do believe in, by the way—loves everybody equally, why do some people have so much while others are barely surviving?"

Walter doesn't reply. (Not that Shelbi was expecting him to.)

"Needless to say, I'm really struggling with driving around in a luxury import I've done nothing to deserve when I know there are over a billion people, some of whom work tirelessly, yet live on like four hundred and fifty dollars a *year*."

They lapse back into silence. Which, in this moment, Shelbi is glad for. Because it's hitting her hard: talking to Walter really *does* feel good, and she *could* use an actual friend her age.

Something she won't tell Walter (not yet anyway): She gave up on the whole *friends* thing a couple years ago. Pretty much all her old friends bailed the first time she went inpatient. And even after she transferred to a new school in LA once she received her diagnosis, she never bothered trying to make new ones.

Well . . . except for one time. And that didn't go so great.

"So what'd you do to get past it?" Walter says then. "The whole crisis thing? 'Cause I think I might be having one."

Shelbi sighs. "This is going to sound really corny, so you have to promise you won't make fun."

"I won't."

"Well, there's this thing called the Serenity Prayer? *'Serenity to accept what I can't change, courage to change what I can, and wisdom to know the difference.'* I've been working with my therapist on it since I moved here."

"You have a therapist?"

Shelbi's pulse picks up—sometimes people get weird

when they find out you have a therapist—but she tries to ignore it. "I do," she says. "Does that bother you?"

Walter snorts. "Not at all. I'm sure *I* could use one. But Cris Criddle doesn't really believe in that sort of thing."

Shelbi has no idea what to say to that. So she checks her watch. "Dang, it's late," she says. "Sorry to cut this short." Which is true but also not. She could use some more time with him to process things. But she's also super uncomfortable now. "I gotta get home."

"Understood." He stands and reaches out a hand to help her up, and once she's on her feet, he smiles down at her. "I really appreciate you hanging out with me, Shelbi."

"You're really tall" is what comes out of Shelbi's mouth in reply. (*So* smooth.)

He like . . . *guffaws* is the word that comes to mind. "Or maybe you're just . . . not?"

"Hey now, I'm starting to like you. Don't ruin it."

Another smile from him. It makes Shelbi nervous that she likes seeing that smile so much.

"May I escort you to your vehicle, madam?" He extends an elbow.

Shelbi looks at Walter's arm for a moment, then exhales and lifts her chin. "I would be absolutely delighted, kind sir."

And off they go.

This graduation is the worst, by the way.

And just so you know, I still think it's utter bullcrap that you're not allowed to be here.

Well hello to you too.

And ¯_(ツ)_/¯

Like fine: you messed up and aren't allowed to give the salutatorian address.

But banning you from even being in the building??

Totally feel like you could take that to the Supreme Court or something.

Lol. I don't think that's entirely necessary. But I appreciate your support.

How are you even texting me right now? Has the ceremony not started?

Oh it started all right. Valedictorian is blathering on about failure.

As if she's ever experienced any . . .

Hey now. Be nice. It's not her fault I decided to drive drunk.

Yeah, well whatever. You should be here is all I'm saying.

Welp, gotta go. They're starting to call names.

Well congratulations to you, Shelbi Camille Augustine.

Still can't believe I actually told you my middle name.

I'll catch you later, okay?

I can hardly wait, you graduate.

GRADUCATION.

And when Quantavious saw the golden-brown curls
and blue eyes of Tay-Tay's redbone baby, he knew:
that little girl wasn't his.
The White Gangsta had struck again.

So goes the end of *Cookies and Cream*, book one in Shonda Crenshaw's White Gangsta series and Andy's chosen "vacation" read. When Shelbi hit him this morning during the graduation ceremony he wasn't allowed to attend, part of him wanted to tell her right then that he was reading one of her mom's books.

He'd just gotten to the part where Connor—aka the White Gangsta—found Tay-Tay sitting outside in the rain after her boyfriend Quantavious kicked her out because he claimed she was cheating (ahem . . . guy had guilty conscience). But Andy decided to wait until he'd finished the whole book.

The time has come.

Shelbi?   he texts her.

Ten seconds . . . thirty . . . sixty . . . two minutes . . . three . . .

No response.

And now Andy's parents are fighting. He can hear them through the sheets of cardboard the owners of this "bed 'n' breakfast" call *walls*.

It's gotten worse, the fighting. Well, when Mom is actually around. She spends a lot of time these days at what was once Andy's grandpa's house but now serves as her campaign headquarters. Honestly, the distance is fine with him. He doesn't even like being in the same room with her at this point. She's gotten so critical of everything.

Dad is playing the good-sport role and attending all of her functions to keep their marital problems out of the press, but Andy is sure it's wearing on him. Especially considering Dad feels the *opposite* way of just about everything Mom claims to stand for.

Frankly, Andy has no idea how his parents wound up married to each other. Dad's a good guy. Andy used to resent the old man for reasons he didn't understand, but now that he's gotten older, Andy realizes he was picking up on the little digs Mom would whisper about Dad when she thought Andy wasn't listening. And since Andy has always wanted to make Mom happy—something he *still* doesn't understand—he basically accepted whatever she said as gospel.

But now that he's seen how . . . unsatisfiable she can be—especially since Emma died—Andy has really grown to appreciate Charles Andrew Criddle. He just wishes he knew how to tell the guy.

Andy's phone buzzes, and he sits up too fast. Smacks his head on the underside of the top bunk in his joke of a room. It's made for small kids: The bunk bed is shaped like a castle, and there's a slide coming down from the top. The room's walls are painted to make it look like a fairy-tale forest, and there's also a plastic rocking horse— a knight's trusty steed, perhaps?—and a mostly flat bean-bag chair shaped like a dragon.

What an experience.

He rubs his throbbing forehead and opens the message:

> Walty Wal-Wal? ;)

Man. It's like a cool breeze on a hot day, that text, and just like that, the sound of Andy's parents fighting be-comes little more than easily ignored background noise.

> So? How was the rest of grad?

> Wack. Salutatorian bailed . . .

> Salutatorian got banned, remember? DUI

> I still think it's absurd.

> Lol crime is crime, Shelbi.

Yeah, yeah, yeah. Whatever. So where even are you?

Some yee-haw town near GA/FL line

Random

"No town w/ registered voters is too small for a campaign visit," said the congresswoman.

Haha! Bored?

Nope. Just finished reading Cookies and Cream.

There's a looooong pause.

Shelbi? You still there?

You didn't.

Oh I did. Think u could get me an author autograph?

No for real, cut it out.

Connor was . . . virile.

You did NOT read that book, Walter!!!

Absolutely hated Quantavious. Totally knew Tay-Tay's baby wasn't his.

AND between the two of us, I was glad because that clown does NOT deserve her.

I cannot believe you read that book. This is so embarrassing!

Why? Your mom is talented!

Walter, my mom's books are utter smut.

English please?

Lol, "smut" = garbage, trash, filth, take your pick.

One man's trash is another man's treasure.

LOL!!!

And now Andy's feeling good because she's laughing out loud in ALL CAPS with triple exclamation. In fact, he's feeling White-Gangsta-Connor-gets-the-girl kind of good.

Walter?

Yesssss?

I need to ask you something.

Okay . . .

Don't get mad, all right?

Hmm . . .

Lol. That doesn't sound good . . .

Walter, are you gay?

And now Andy's hearing the *boooooop* sound in his ear that lets him know he's dialed her number and the line is ringing.

"Oh gosh, are you mad?" she says the moment she picks up.

"No, I'm not mad, I just—umm . . ."

Maybe he should've waited a couple of minutes to collect his thoughts. Because they're jumbled. And he's struggling to put together a sentence.

"Well?" she says.

"Well, what?"

"Are you?"

Andy smacks his forehead. "No, Shelbi. I'm not gay."

"Oh."

(*What does she mean* Oh?!) "Why do you sound so disappointed?"

"I'm not *disappointed* . . . I just—I wanted to know. You know I'd be fine with it if you were, right?"

"Shelbi, you took me to see *RENT.* I know you'd be fine with it. Seriously, though: I'm not gay."

"Okay."

There's another awkward pause. Did she really think Andy was gay?! Does he *seem* gay? "Why'd you ask?"

"Huh?"

"What made you think I was gay?"

"Oh . . . The way you responded to the musical was a little jarring? And you never really said *why* you were so impacted. Then I thought about your mom and her 'views' or whatever. I knew you *had* an ex-girlfriend, but I didn't know why you'd broken up. And I guess . . . I dunno. It seemed possible?"

Now Andy has to laugh. "Seriously?"

"I mean, what else was I supposed to think?"

Is this conversation really happening? "It was about Angel."

"Huh?"

"The whole thing with *RENT.* It mostly had to do with what happened to Angel. I uhh . . . I lost someone earlier this year."

"Oh, wow. I was *way* off. I'm so sorry."

Andy sighs. "It's cool. But yeah: messed me up real good."

"Guessing you don't want to talk about it?"

"Not really," Andy says, relieved at the out. "If . . . that's okay."

"Of course it is. We never have to talk about anything you don't want to."

Except now they need something *else* to talk about. Because Andy is definitely not ready to hang up.

"So what about you?" he says. "Are *you* gay?"

Though Andy is appalled at his boldness—*Who does he think he even* is *right now?*—the laugh that fills his ear literally makes the tension melt from his shoulders. "Depends on your definition," she replies. "Not everyone defines it the same way, you know."

Andy . . . didn't actually know that. But before he can say so, she's speaking again.

"You wanna tell me what happened with your ex? You

know, since you guys didn't break up because you're secretly gay."

(The way this girl makes Andy laugh is astonishing.)

"Her name was Stephanie," he begins. "We dated ninth grade through last summer—"

But then he stops. And just as he does, he hears Mom shout something unintelligible before a door slams so hard, one of the framed dragon pictures pops off the wall in his castle room.

His mind clouds over as the ugly circumstances of his and Steph's demise bust their way to the forefront of his memory. Yet another reason Andy's got issues with the congresswoman.

He swallows down what he was going to tell Shelbi. "It didn't work out" is all he says.

"So now you're waiting for the *right* one."

"You could say that," he replies, thankful she seemed to take the hint and didn't pry. "Though I'm *perfectly* fine with being unattached." *And never going through anything like that again,* he thinks.

"Got it."

There's another pause, but this time, it's comfortable. Organic.

"Hey, Walter?" she says.

"Yeah?"

"Thank you for not getting mad."

"About you asking if I'm gay?"

"Yeah."

"Well, for what it's worth, I don't think I *can* get mad at you, Shelbi." And Andy instantly wishes he could take that back because it sounded really sappy. Stephanie didn't like that sort of thing. "I mean—" *Backtrack, Criddle.* "You've been such a good friend to me these past couple weeks. I really appreciate it."

Shelbi doesn't respond, and *this* pause regresses to awkward. As it stretches across the seconds, Andy wonders if his mushiness killed the mood. And now he's a little mad at himself for not holding it in.

But then she speaks: "You consider this a friendship?"

And Andy has no idea what to do with that.

"Uhhh . . . Yes?" *Is he giving the wrong answer?* "Should I consider it something else?"

"No . . . a friendship is fine," Shelbi replies. But she doesn't sound sure. (Which Andy finds *very* confusing.)

"Listen, I have to run," she says then. "When are you coming back?"

"Tomorrow."

"Okay. Let me know when you're home, all right?"

"All right . . ." *What on earth just happened?*

"Bye, Walter." She hangs up.

And since Andy's parents aren't yelling anymore, he's engulfed in silence. Back to sitting alone in the dungeon of his castle bunk bed, staring at a deflated dragon.

And wishing, more than anything, that he had access to a drink.

Becky.

Shelbi has chewed her nails to nubs. Something she hasn't done in like . . . six months. She's called her beloved cousin four times in the past twenty-three minutes, but she's not answering.

Yes, Becky is one of the few people who has never treated Shelbi like one of those wildly ornate, precious-gemstone-covered eggs that no one will handle without gloves on—hence her having no problem missing Shelbi's phone calls. But if there was one time Shelbi wished Becky would treat every call like an emergency, this is it.

Is the nail-biting freakout an overreaction? Absolutely. She feels like there's a battle between nuclear fusion and fission going on inside her chest, and she's fully aware—intellectually—that her brain's hyper-panicked response doesn't actually fit the circumstances.

But the first thing that popped into her mind when she heard Walter say *friend* . . . wasn't spectacular. Yes, it *has* occurred to her that she could use a "friend." But in reality, she hasn't exactly recovered from what happened the last time she allowed herself to get attached to someone her age (who she's not related to).

Her phone rings.

She rushes over to her desk to grab it and winds up

knocking it onto the floor. As she squats to pick it up, she realizes how intensely her hands are shaking.

She slides her fingertip across the screen and turns on the speakerphone. "Hello?"

"Hey, girl," a voice says.

"Becky?"

"Oh Lord. Somebody's in crisis," Becky replies. "What happened?"

Shelbi takes a deep breath. "Walter said we're in a 'friendship.'"

"Umm . . . who is Walter?"

"This boy from school."

"Mmmmm . . . You sure it's not one of your toothless buddies at the old folks' home? *Walter* ain't exactly a high schooler's name, boo."

"Can you be serious for like *five* seconds?"

"Nope," Becky replies. "Somebody's gotta relax around here, considering how seriously *you're* taking things."

Shelbi sighs. "Okay, fine. You're right."

"Now take a few of those prada-vaka breaths—"

"*Pranayama.*"

"You clearly knew what I meant, so your little correction was wholly unnecessary." (Shelbi can practically *hear* her favorite cousin roll her eyes.) "Just take some and then tell me what's wrong."

So Shelbi does. She heads over to the bed and lies on her back, then inhales deep . . . deeper . . . deeper . . . before letting it go.

And then again.

And again.

She sits up and puts the phone to her ear. "Okay, that was pretty helpful."

"What would you do without me, Cuz?" Becky says. "Now what's up?"

"I just . . . well, he doesn't *know*."

"Doesn't know *what*?" Becky asks.

"About *me*. And, you know, my thing—"

"When are you going to stop calling it that?"

"When people stop thinking you're 'crazy' when they hear you have it?"

"That's backwards af, just so you know. But Imma let you finish."

"Thank you," Shelbi says. "Anyway, it was galactically uncomfortable hearing him call me a 'friend' when he knows pretty much nothing about me. Well, other than the fact that Shonda 'Smut Queen' Crenshaw is my mom."

"And you think it would change things if he knew more?"

"I have no idea."

In the pause Becky draaaags out—100 percent for effect—Shelbi knows exactly what her beloved cousin is about to say.

"I mean you could just—"

"—tell him and see what happens?" Shelbi finishes.

"You said it, not me."

"Man, I hate when you do that."

"But do you *really*, Shelli Belli?" Becky says. "Because

I'm pretty sure this is the precise trajectory of just about every phone conversation we have."

Shelbi doesn't respond.

"I mean, do you *want* to be his friend?" Becky asks.

"Well, that's the thing . . . So there's this phenomenon in space where—"

"Oh boy, here we go. Do I need to pull out my encyclopedia?"

"Just hush and listen," Shelbi says. "So sometimes two separate stars will orbit a common center of mass, which binds them together by gravitational forces. If they're close enough together, they can exchange stellar material. It's called a binary star system. And I just feel like maybe Walter and I have something like that going on?"

"It's like you're making these strange sounds, but I have no idea what they mean."

"Oh, shut up."

Becky laughs. "The answer was yes, you do want to be friends. So you know what you gotta do. For your *own* conscience."

"And if he can't handle it, he can't handle it. Right?"

"Correct. And good riddance."

Which leaves Shelbi with only one thing to figure out: how to tell him.

AGREEMENT.

Andy was pretty smashed when Shelbi texted last night, but he apparently managed to pick up on tomorrow morning at 10:30 because here he is: dragging himself out of bed and into the shower, despite a headache that feels like there's an axe embedded in his skull.

Not that he has any idea where they're going. Also doesn't have it in him to ask once he's in the car beside Shelbi and they're on the way.

Which is something Andy comes to regret: a third of the way up what he learns is Shelbi's weekly hike to the top of Stone Mountain, he wishes he'd known this was what she had planned. Because he would've *definitely* said no. It's only a mile from the base to the 1,686-foot peak, but by the time they reach the top, he's sweated about four buckets and smells like a wet horse. It's dead obvious that he's been slacking on his judo training.

"You all right there, Ninja-boy?" Shelbi drops her backpack to the ground and gives Andy a gentle shove, but he's so out of breath, she might as well have pushed him with the force of ten men. He totally stumbles.

"Obviously not a ninja." He shuts his eyes as a perfectly timed breeze hits his face—which is very likely sunburnt. "Ninjas are in shape, and I obviously am not."

Shelbi laughs the laugh that makes the sun shine brighter, so Andy looks her way. She has commenced a stretching routine. In this moment, he can see her right side, and she's bent over at the waist in her yoga pants with both palms flat on the mountaintop.

He'd made it a point to hike in *front* of her on the way up—partially because he couldn't let her *beat* him, but also because he's been trying to keep it respectful. However, there is no denying that Shelbi is very . . . *fit*. She's not exceptionally large in the chest region or anything, but her lower half is a force to be reckoned with. As White Gangsta Connor puts it in *Cookies and Cream*, "dat ass is enough to make a grown man cry." (Andy really hopes Shelbi can't read minds.)

She moves into an inner-thigh stretch—Andy's quite thankful she's doing all this with her eyes closed because he's certainly staring at this point—then brings her feet together and stretches both arms up over her head. Her tank top lifts, revealing the warm brown skin of her waist and a series of parallel scars there. Two are completely visible, but there's a third peeking out from the top of her pants, and a fourth just beneath the edge of her shirt.

"Dang it!" she says, yanking her shirt down when she opens her eyes and catches Andy looking. "You weren't supposed to see those yet."

Uhhh . . . "Yet?"

"Yeah. I planned to show you once we started getting into my history," she says. "Guess we'll speed things up a bit."

"Okay . . ."

Shelbi grabs the backpack she brought with her, and from within it, she produces a thin blanket, a thermos, two cups, and a couple of Tupperware containers. "Let's eat," she says, passing Andy one.

He sits beside her on the blanket and opens it. Inside there's a grilled chicken breast on a bed of brown rice, sliced carrot sticks, and a second, smaller container of mixed berries. While Andy's marveling at the *classiness* of the contents (*This is a picnic lunch?*), something else appears in his line of sight. A blue folder.

He looks up at Shelbi.

"Yeah, I know: this feels bizarre," she says. "But we need to discuss . . . some things."

"Some things?"

"About me. Feel free to, umm, read at your leisure. While we eat."

Shelbi gets very focused on her Tupperware once Andy removes the folder from her grasp. Curious—and vaguely terrified?—he opens it.

There's what looks like some sort of contract on one side and a folded brochure on the other: BIPOLAR 101: HOW TO SUPPORT A CHILD OR TEEN LIVING WITH BIPOLAR DEPRESSION. He pulls that out first. Inside is an explanation of what bipolar depression is, the types, lists of symptoms for different episodes, a list of the conditions that can occur *with* the various classifications of the disorder, the brain structure and functions involved, treatment options, and then the entire back side is dedicated to tips for caregivers and family members.

Shelbi clears her throat, and Andy's head snaps up.

"Sorry," she says. "Didn't mean to startle you. Just . . . wanted to make sure you also read the other thing in the folder."

So Andy tucks the brochure back in and pulls the sheet of paper out.

FRIENDSHIP AGREEMENT

I, _____, on this ___ day of _____, as regards entry into a formal friendship with Shelbi Camille Augustine, knowingly and willfully agree to abide by the terms set forth below.

1. The use of any and all mental illness slurs—cuckoo, ("cuckchoo," "for Cocoa Puffs," etc.), cray, cray-cray, crazy, crazy pants, nuts, nutty, nutjob, wackjob, whackadoodle, off her rocker, deranged, basket case, head case, mental case, insane ("in the membrane"), spaz, loon(ey), yahoo, fruitcake, demented, crackpot, loca, lunatic, meshuggah, lost her marbles, "bipolar" (used derogatorily), etc.—is strictly prohibited.

2. Don't make fun. Ever.

3. If you sense "out of the ordinary" behavior, you may ask Shelbi how she is doing, but don't get

awkward and start looking for symptoms that aren't there.

4. Along those lines, if Shelbi confirms that she is dealing with an episode, don't take any action that will exacerbate things or be the opposite of helpful. This includes, but is not limited to: encouraging risky behavior; exposing her to known triggers (this includes in conversation); being overtly unkind; telling her to "cheer up" or "calm down" or "relax" or "think positive." (Trust: if it were that simple, she wouldn't be having an episode.)

5. If it becomes too much to handle, be forthright and friend-break-up with Shelbi. She's dealt with people bailing before and can handle it, but isn't a fan of being ghosted.

6. Do not, under any circumstances, fall in love with Shelbi.

Andy clears his throat. "Number six is a bit bold, don't you think?"

Shelbi won't look him in the eye. "Just making sure I cover all my bases. I'm settled in who I am and how my brain works, but in my experience, people can get weird. Especially when *those* kinds of feelings get involved. And romance really isn't my thing, so best to lay it out up front."

"Ah."

"Being forthright here, I don't really have any *friends*. The only person my age I interact with regularly is my cousin. And though I haven't had a serious episode in sixteen and a half months, the last one was a doozie and was triggered by something that happened with a 'friend.' I'd prefer to never go through anything like that again. Hence the whole *agreement* thing."

Andy is quiet for a few seconds, and then he says: "What are they like? Your episodes, I mean."

And to his surprise, she smiles. "Glad you asked. That's partially why I brought you up here. So I could explain with a visual metaphor."

Andy almost laughs: from what he's learned about her so far, this is definitely a Shelbi Augustine thing to do. "Okay," he says. "I'm listening."

She shifts her gaze into the distance. "Look out there. Everything seems all peaceful and serene, right?"

It does. "Right."

"Well, we're approximately two thousand three hundred and thirty-two miles north of the equator. *At* the equator, the earth is rotating at just over a thousand miles per hour." She looks at Andy. "Do you know what would happen if it suddenly stopped spinning?"

Andy thinks for a second and realizes this is something he never would've thought to even consider. "No. But I definitely want to know now."

Shelbi laughs. "Well, in a nutshell, because of inertia,

the atmosphere and oceans would continue to move at over a thousand miles per hour. Which would equal a natural disaster unlike any this planet has ever seen."

"Okay . . ."

"It'd be like the biggest, baddest, most epic tsunami and an ultra-supersonic wind happening simultaneously across the globe. Everything rooted would be ripped from the earth—buildings, trees, even mountains, including this mini one we're sitting on. And anything that moves—people, vehicles, animals, et cetera—would just fly off the ground like blown bits of eraser dust."

"Dang. That sounds . . . Yeah, I don't really know what to say to that."

"That's what an episode feels like for me," she says. "My whole world stops dead, but everything around me keeps going. I get thrown into this, like, emotional cataclysm and feel completely out of control."

They're quiet for a minute, and then Shelbi shifts to her knees. She lifts her shirt and lowers the waistband of her shorts to expose her right side. There are nine almost perfectly parallel scars, each about an inch wide: the topmost is right at the bottom of her rib cage and the lowest is on her hip. Taken together, they look like the rungs of a ladder. "I know you caught a peek of these earlier, but I wanted you to see them all," she says.

Without thinking, Andy reaches out and run his fingertips over them, completely in awe. His old sensei's voice pops into his head: *Scars exist to remind us of what we've survived.* Shelbi has apparently survived quite a bit.

When he looks up at her, she's staring at him very much in shock. And that's when he realizes what he's doing and snatches his hand back. "Crap. Sorry," he says.

A little cloud of tension forms as she sits back down. "Umm, no worries."

But then she doesn't say anything else.

"You were . . . talking about the world stopping?"

"Oh. Yeah." She seems to shake herself back to reality. "So all of those scars on my side came from that out-of-control feeling."

"Got it," Andy says. And yes: he's a little shocked. But not nearly as shocked—or panicked?—as he would've thought he'd be. He's obviously *heard* of self-harm, but Shelbi's the first person he's ever met who's actually dealt with it.

"I'll spare you the details," she goes on, "but I will say this: You have highs and lows in your moods, right?"

Andy nods. "Sure do."

"Correct. Because everyone does. Mine are just exacerbated. My highs aren't *super* high like you see on bad TV shows and movies, but when I drop, it happens really hard and really fast. My first episode hit three years ago. I was thirteen, and had an aunt I was super close to: Aunt Shannon. She was *un*diagnosed—my granny, Mom's mom, is one of those women who swears mental illness only happens to white people, and prayer is the only 'medicine' anyone needs—"

"Sounds familiar," Andy says as Mom-of-the-Year Cris Criddle's face pops into his head. "Sorry for cutting you off."

"No problem. I figured you would get it. Anyway, my grandmother never took my aunt Shannon to see anyone when she would have her 'fits,' as Granny called them. Don't ever use that term, by the way."

"Duly noted."

"Thank you. Long story short here, Aunt Shannon took her own life when I was a freshman. And I plummeted into a depression that was like nothing I'd ever experienced."

"That sounds awful."

Shelbi nods. "I wound up in the hospital, it was so bad. The doctors started me on medication, but that particular one wound up swinging me too far in the opposite direction. This is when that whole DUI/MIP thing happened," she says.

"Okay . . ."

"My parents could tell something was up—well . . . *besides* my blood-alcohol content—so they took me back to the hospital. Took like a month and a half, but I eventually landed on the right medication combo. I changed schools, got resettled, and things were solid for almost a year."

"Well, that's good, right?"

"Yes, but then the season changed, and I experienced my first mixed episode."

"Mixed—"

"You can read about it in the brochure. Don't wanna get into it right now," she says. "At any rate, someone who was supposed to be a 'friend' did some very *unfriendly* things."

"Hmph," Andy grunts. "I don't even know what happened, and I'm ready to kick this person's ass."

Shelbi laughs. Like *loud*. Whatever tension was there bursts and flutters away like the confetti from a party popper. "Well, I guess on the bright side, that whole thing landed me *here*. I homeschooled for a while, then my mom—who thankfully is not like *her* mom—found this therapist/psychiatrist duo who are known for their collaborative work with teenagers. And since we already had family in Atlanta, it was a no-brainer."

"And you've been episode-free for sixteen months now, you said?"

"Correct," Shelbi says. "You're a pretty solid listener, Mr. Criddle."

"Mr. Criddle is my *grandfather*, thank you very much."

More laughter. (Mission accomplished.)

It's quiet for a moment, but comfortably so. Shelbi seems . . . relieved.

A cool breeze rushes over them, and Andy takes in the scene around them in light of everything she just shared.

"So . . . you still wanna be friends?" she says, breaking the silence.

"Of course," Andy replies. "What kind of question is that, Shelbi?"

"I was kidding. Mostly."

They meet eyes. Number six from the agreement crosses

Andy's mind, but he shoves it away. "So, you got a pen? I didn't exactly think to bring one on, you know, our hike up a mountain?"

"As a matter of fact I *do*." She produces one from her bag, and he gets to scribbling. Hopefully she can read his handwriting.

"What are you doing?" she asks.

"Adding an amendment."

"What?"

He holds the sheet out to her.

7. Shelbi must always be her true self. No holds barred.

"Deal?" he asks.

She takes the pen and puts her initials by the amendment. "Deal."

"Great."

Andy winks and adds his signature.

Shels?

You awake?

I am now 😊

Good morning.

Oh, sorry about that.

Good morning.

Did you . . . sleep okay?

Yeah, I guess.

Walter?

Yeah?

It's 6:43 am.

In the summertime.

You are correct.

So what's the matter?

Huh?

Well as I've mentioned before: dimpled baby face does not = born yesterday.

This is clearly a text SOS.

Mmmm . . . Potentially?

Get dressed. Workout clothes.

I'll be outside in 14 minutes.

Piloga.

Shelbi *knows* she and Walter are friends for real now . . . She brought him to her most beloved place and had him join her most sacred activity: piloga (aka Pilates + yoga) atop Arabia Mountain.

"You know," he huffs (the guy's totally out of breath), "I've been in the Atlanta area my whole life and had no idea there were so many mountains to climb." He drops down onto his yoga mat and takes a swig from the water bottle Shelbi packed for him. "Also, I can understand you wanting to torture me, but calling it *paloka* or whatever is just rude." He swigs again. "If not for this water, I'd likely be dead."

"*Piloga*," Shelbi corrects. "Get it right. And I guess it's a good thing I *brought* you the water. You're welcome, by the way."

Not that she thinks either of them will ever mention it, but Walter left *his* water bottle in her car after their Stone Mountain hike a few days ago. When Shelbi went to wash it, she discovered that it was definitely *not* filled with water. She'd dumped the contents and tossed the bottle itself in her family's recycling bin.

"Man, that was intense," he says, wiping his brow. "You work out a lot, huh?"

At this, Shelbi smiles. Having her athletic prowess acknowledged makes her feel pretty dang good. "Exercise helps me stay steady," she says. "Endorphins and stuff. Don't you feel better?"

"You know, now that you mention it, I really do."

"Excellent," she says. "So?"

Walter looks at her like he's about to say *So what?* But then he . . . doesn't. Just drops his eyes and takes what is clearly a *very* deep breath. "I'm sick of pretending like everything is hunky-dory."

"Thrilled to hear it, Walty."

His head snaps up. "*Walty?!*"

"Just roll with it." She pats his leg. "You were saying?"

She watches as his face clouds over. "When I texted you this morning, I was in my bathroom with the shower turned on, trying to drown out the sound of my mom saying I'm not her son anymore and calling me an alcoholic."

"Are you?" Shelbi asks.

"Am I what?"

"An alcoholic."

"Of course not," Walter says. (The answer comes a bit *too* quick, but Shelbi doesn't say anything.) "Like, yes: I drink sometimes when I get overwhelmed. But I could also just . . . not. Like, it's something I *choose* to do."

"Okay," Shelbi says with a shrug. She's certainly heard that one before . . .

"You believe me, don't you?" he asks. Which Shelbi isn't expecting.

She answers honestly: "Depends on whether or not *you* believe you, Walter." She looks him in the eye. "Do you?"

He actually pauses to think this time. Which is a good sign. "Yes," he says. "I do believe me."

"Great. Then I believe you too. Feel free to continue. You were talking about your mom saying mean things."

"Right," Walter says. "Well, she was arguing with my dad, who was defending my 'actions' on account of my grief. Not sure if you know, but my baby sister died back in March. Her name was Emma."

"Wow. I'm really sorry to hear that, Wal."

"Thanks. Anyway, Mom and Dad have been at each other's throats for months now. Those smiles you see on TV and in pictures are the *furthest* thing from reality."

"You know, I kind of figured that," Shelbi replies. "Your dad has a lot of sadness in his eyes."

"Yeah. At this point, Mom spends more time at her 'campaign headquarters' than at home, and . . . I dunno. It's like ever since my granddad died last year, she's been insatiable."

"Insatiable?"

"Literally. It's impossible to satisfy her at this point. She's pushed me pretty hard my whole life, but now nothing *anybody* does is satisfactory. And don't *dare* make a mistake."

Shelbi watches Walter's Adam's apple bob, and on instinct, she scooches closer to him and puts her head on his shoulder. She can feel some of his tension release.

"You wanna know what I heard her say right before I went into the bathroom?"

"Tell me."

"She said, 'If Andrew had been more diligent, we might still *have* Emma.'"

At this, Shelbi sits up. Like what even kind of mom—"She *said* that?"

Andy nods and his head drops again "Worst part is she's right."

"No, Walter." She's tempted to lift his chin and turn his face toward her. But she resists. "That's a god-awful thing to say, and she is *not* right."

"But she is, though, Shelbi. The whole thing was my fault."

"How?"

Walter takes a deep breath. "We went to the Bahamas for spring break this year, and our bungalow had its own pool right off the patio," he says, surprising Shelbi with how open he is willing to be. "My parents had gone out and I was supposed to be babysitting Emma . . ."

He stops.

Again, on instinct, Shelbi shifts her body so she can wrap her arms around Walter's waist.

Which is when he dissolves. "I fell asleep, Shelbi. I fell asleep, and Emma got outside. My mom's scream is what woke me up. By the time I got to the patio door, my dad was performing CPR, but her skin was like . . . I could tell it was too late. Sorry, that's really morbid."

"It's okay."

"She was only three years old," he says. "Sorry for crying, by the way."

"I swear on everything, I will fight you if you ever apologize for crying again," Shelbi says.

Walter laughs. "I think we both know you wouldn't win that one. But okay."

"Just continue your story, please and thank you."

She feels him shrug. "I mean there's nothing else to say. To this day, I've got all these 'if-onlys' running around in my head. If only I hadn't fallen asleep; if only I'd made sure the door was locked; if only I'd taught her how to swim."

Shelbi lets him go and returns to her mat beside him. (Largely because she was getting a bit *too* comfortable with the contact.)

"I just can't believe I was *sleeping*," he says. "While my baby sister was probably crying and thrashing and choking, I was taking a damn *nap*."

"But why?" Shelbi asks.

"Why what?"

"I mean, you *clearly* loved your sister, Walter. If you fell asleep while watching her, there had to be a reason you were so tired."

He shrugs. "I hadn't really slept the night before."

"Why not?"

"Well, my parents were fighting, and it made Emma upset. So she came and slept in my bed. I already had a lot on my mind, and she was kind of a thrasher, so I didn't sleep at all."

"What were they fighting about?"

Now Walter snorts. "What *weren't* they fighting about?" he says. "I told you, my mom's been a monster since her dad died. Which is kind of ironic because *he* was a monster when he was alive."

"Hmm."

"What does *hmm* mean?"

"I'm just putting some pieces together," Shelbi says. "You said Emma's death is your fault, right? Because you fell asleep."

"Yeah . . ."

"Okay. Well then, it's also her *own* fault. Because she's the reason you hadn't slept the night before and were therefore sleepy."

It's almost like she can *feel* his mood shift instantly. "*Excuse—*"

"Hold on, I'm not done." Shelbi puts a hand up. "Hear me out, please."

He wraps his arms around his knees. "All right. Go on."

"It's also your parents' fault because they upset her to the point where she came to you. Which makes it also your grandpa's fault since your mom changed when *he* died."

"Okay . . ."

"And it's no one fault that your grandpa died because that's what old people do at some point. So, what I'm getting at here is that if Emma's death is your fault, it's also everyone's fault and no one's fault." She turns to him. "You get what I'm saying?"

"Mmmm . . ."

"The fault chain never ceases, Walter. Yeah, life's a whole lot of cause and effect, but every cause *was* an effect at some point." It's quiet for a moment . . . during which Shelbi finds herself looking at Walter's hand and wanting to take it in her own. "You know why I brought you here?" she says, trying to shake herself out of it.

"Why?"

"Because of the vastness." She gestures all around and up at the sky. "Here, there's really nothing between earth and sky. I consider this my rendezvous point with the universe."

"Hey, Shelbi?" he says, breaking her trance.

"Yes?"

"You're a real nerd, you know that?"

"Oh my God, I can't stand you." And she smacks his upper arm. His very *strong* and *toned* upper arm.

He just laughs. "Seriously, though, not to get all sappy, but you're kind of a godsend."

If Shelbi's skin was a *smidge* less brown, Walter would surely see her blushing. She dusts her hands off (wholly unnecessarily). "Come," she says, standing up.

"Come where?"

"You need a hug," she says. "Friends give friends hugs when they need them, don't they?" She grabs Walter's hands and pulls him to his feet. Then she rises onto her tiptoes and wraps her arms around his neck.

It's like hugging a tree trunk at first (*Has this boy never hugged a girl before?!*), but he's warm and solid. Shelbi can tell the moment he relaxes because his (strong) arms circle her waist and then her feet are leaving the ground.

It's kind of a lot.

"You were right," he says against her collarbone. "I did need a hug. Also, you smell pretty good for a person who just hiked *and* did an hour of paloma."

"It's *piloga*, you imbecile!"

He laughs, and Shelbi can feel it in her chest. (Literally.)

Maybe she *could* get used to this whole friendship thing.

PHASE 2

Protostar Formation

AUGUSTINES.

Yesterday, when Shelbi broke the news that her parents wanted Andy to come over for dinner, he got excited.

He'd spent the morning beneath the soured glare of a grumpy old judge who, in addition to the six-month license suspension and forty hours of community service Andy expected, smacked him with a twelve-month probation sentence. Mom attempted to pay it off—"Can't have a son on probation during an election," she'd grumbled to the lawyer—but Judge Grump wasn't having it.

When Andy got home—after being trapped in the car, completely sober, with crotchety Congresswoman Cris Criddle for forty-eight minutes—he read book two in the White Gangsta series, *Rich White Chocolate*, as a pick-me-up. So the idea of getting to meet *the* Shonda Crenshaw had him ready to jump out of his skin.

Now, though? As the big black Benz—which was sent to pick him up—winds its way toward the massive pink mansion he's only ever seen from behind, it hits him: he has no idea what the hell he's gotten himself into.

The car stops, and Mario looks at Andy in the rearview mirror and says "Stay put" before exiting the vehicle himself. (Not at *all* terrifying. Nope. Not one bit.)

Then Andy's car door is opening from the outside, and Mario is gesturing for him to get out and head to the front door of the house. *Doors.* Of the house. Because there are two of them. And they are massive.

They both fly open before his finger hits the intercom button. And there before Andy stands a dark-skinned woman with a short, nutmeg-colored Afro.

Shonda. Freaking. Crenshaw. (Aaaand, he's kind of freaking out a little bit on the inside.)

Her high heels make her extra tall, but she's really graceful, and way prettier than the author photo on her books. She brings her hands together beneath her chin, revealing long, cotton-candy-pink fingernails and enough jewelry to pay for Andy's undergraduate education. "Walter!" she coos.

"You can't call him that, Mama!" Shelbi yells from somewhere within the recesses of the bastion. Andy has no idea how she even *heard* her mom, but it makes him smile.

Shonda Crenshaw rolls her eyes. "That child . . . ," she says. "Come on in, young man."

So he does.

The first thing to be said about the interior of the Augustine domain is that the walls are all hung with paintings of Black people in various states of undress. Andy's glad Shonda Crenshaw is walking in front of him because he totally blushes as they pass a sculpture of two naked figures entwined in a position that would result in a pregnancy were the people alive.

When they step into the kitchen—which is three times the size of the Criddle kitchen—there's a large, bespectacled man with Shelbi's warm brown skin tone and thick, wavy hair leaning over the central island. Without a doubt, Shelbi's dad. When he sees them, the man rises to his full height, and it takes everything in Andy not to stumble backward. "You must be Andrew," he rumbles in a voice like a clap of thunder. "It's a pleasure to meet you, young man."

Andy gulps and sticks his hand out like he's nowhere near the threshold of wetting himself. "It's great to meet you, too, sir."

He grabs Andy's hand (*ow*), gives it a single pump, and then goes to a cabinet next to the fridge and takes out a glass. "Would you like a scotch?" he asks.

Andy *almost* says yes. Because he very much *would* like a scotch. Or possibly three scotches. If Shelbi's dad has them to spare . . .

"Umm . . . I'm not twenty-one yet, sir," he says instead.

"Good answer!" He turns around and winks at Andy. "I was testing you, son. You passed with flying colors!"

"Daddy, be nice," Shelbi says, sweeping into the room. Her hair is out and big, she's wearing a billowy strapless dress thing that goes down to her ankles, and she's barefoot (blue toenails). She looks . . . *immaculate* is the word that pops into Andy's head. He would very much like to stare at her for a while.

She comes over and gives him side hug. "You look spiffy, Walty-Wal," she says. "I see you're channeling a little Charlie with the rolled sleeves."

About that: not that he'd ever tell anyone, but Charlie

Criddle totally picked out Andy's threads. And ironed them for him. And . . . rolled his sleeves.

Now Shelbi is winking at Andy (winking family, he sees), and he gets this weird fluttery thing in his chest.

Rule number six, Criddle. Pull it together.

"Thank you," he says. "You look really nice too."

Shelbi laughs. "Welcome to me in my element." She does a little twirl and there's no stopping the super-smile that overtakes Andy's face. In his peripheral vision, Andy sees Shelbi's mom watching him with a smirk.

He's gotta switch gears. And fast. "You have a lovely home, Mrs. Augustine."

She smiles, and Andy can see where Shelbi gets the dimples. "You can drop the formalities, Andy. Any friend of Shelbi's is a friend of ours. Call me Shonda—"

"And call *me* Dr. Augustine." Shelbi's dad's laugh brings new meaning to the word *booming.*

Shelbi rolls her eyes. "You're not funny, Daddy . . ."

"Your mama sure thinks I am . . . Ain't that right, baby?" He swats Shelbi's mom on the butt and she giggles and says, "You old dog!" and then they kiss. As much as Andy wants to look away, he can't. Too much in awe of their old-people PDA. He can't recall a single time in the past three years that he's seen his parents kiss without a camera in front of them.

Shelbi scrunches her nose and says, "You guys are nasty."

"Girl, take your behind on, and show your guest to his seat," Shonda says.

Dinner itself gets off to an awkward start. As the salad is being passed around the table (the Augustines have a driver, but they don't have servants), Andy, apparently wanting to impress Shelbi's parents with his dinner-table conversation prowess, says: "So Shonda, I've read a couple of your books."

Once it's past his lips, Andy realizes that maybe wasn't the right thing to say: Dr. Augustine's fork stops halfway to his mouth, and Shelbi spits out her water.

If he'd thought it through, it might've occurred to Andy that eighteen-year-old Ivy League–bound judo black belt Eagle Scouts are very likely not a part of Shonda Crenshaw's typical readership. And perhaps he would've done something sensible like ask Dr. Augustine what it's like to be a neurosurgeon. But alas. Think it through, he did not. And now a silence the size of an African elephant has thudded onto the table.

After a few beats, Shonda cocks her head to the side. "You have?" she says to Andy.

He nods. And then clenches his teeth. He's 98 percent sure of what question is coming next, and dreading it with every fiber of his being . . .

"Which ones?"

And there it is. (*Dear God, please help him.*)

He tosses a grenade into the center of his dignity: "The first two in the White Gangsta series."

Dr. Augustine explodes into belly-quaking laughter, and Andy is reminded of the Kente Claus (read: Black

Santa) his well-meaning white father used to take him to see as a kid.

Shonda is beaming. She clasps her *blinged-out* (White Gangsta–speak for "diamond jewelry–covered") hands on the table and leans forward. "Well, what'd ya think?"

Andy glances around. Every Augustine eye is on him.

Already leapt into the fire . . . might as well dance in it. "I loved them, Shonda. Would it be awful of me to ask for your autograph?"

And now both she and Dr. Augustine are laughing, and Shelbi is shaking her head and trying not to smile (and failing). "So you didn't think Connor was too much?" Shonda continues.

"Well, I mean he's definitely vigorous . . . Certainly seems to have more *endurance* than the average white guy—"

Oh boy . . .

"I mean . . . Not that I know from experience or anything—" Andy puts his head in his hands. "Wow, this is going downhill fast."

At this, Dr. Augustine reaches over and pats Andy on the back. "You're all right, young man," he says, still laughing.

The rest of dinner goes off without a hitch, and afterward there's chocolate cheesecake, college talk, and Cards Against Humanity (Shonda's suggestion, and yes: things get awkward a time or two). Then when it's time for Andy to head home—*probation* equals strict 10:30 p.m. curfew—Dr. Augustine insists that Shelbi drive him.

He smiles the whole way—Shonda handed him a signed

copy of *Cream to My Coffee*, book three in the White Gangsta series, on his way out—but once they're in front of his house and she's putting the car in park, it occurs to Andy that Shelbi hasn't said a word since they *slid* into the supple leather seats.

"You okay?" he asks.

"Hmm?" She looks at him.

"You're pretty quiet over there . . ."

"Oh," she says. "I'm great! Just tired." She forces a smile.

Andy wants to press. He really does. But then he remembers the rule about looking for things that aren't there. So instead, he takes a deep breath and says, "Shelbi, may I have a hug?"

She looks pretty caught off guard, but only for half a second. And when she smiles this time, it's real. "Of course you may, Walter."

They get out and meet in front of the car. She wraps her arms around Andy's neck, and he slips his around her waist and lifts her off her feet like he did when they were at her rendezvous point with the universe. "Thanks for coming to dinner, Walter," she whispers. Her breath is warm against Andy's ear. It makes the dark hairs all over his body stand on end.

"Thank you for having me, Shelbi," he replies (very much struggling to keep his thoughts pure). "It was an honor and a privilege."

He reluctantly puts her down.

Surprise.

Shelbi can't bring herself to get out of the car.

She's been sitting in the garage for seventeen minutes now—shocked, but thankful, that Mama hasn't come out to check on her—thinking back over the wonderful evening, and low-key dreading going in the house.

Why?

> Family meeting when you return, Shelli Belli.

From Daddy. Sent before she even got the car cranked to drive Walter home.

She sighs.

What he doesn't—and will never—know: he'd been invited to dinner because Becks had ratted Shelbi out. A thing Shelbi is still pissed about, by the way.

She'd come down to breakfast the previous morning and immediately been accosted: "So Shels, Becky tells me there's a new boy in your life?" Mama said out of nowhere.

If you ask Shelbi, the approach was quite rude on a number of levels. Especially considering that Daddy was sitting right there. Mama knows how that man is about . . . well, anything pertaining to his "beloved baby girl."

"A boy?" Daddy replied, sitting bolt upright in his chair. You would think based on his reaction that Shelbi had just told them she was pregnant.

The worst part: as soon as Mama decided to announce that Walter is the son of Cris Criddle, Daddy basically lost his whole mind. "That narrow-minded congresswoman?" he said. Then he looked at Shelbi like she had seventeen heads. "You mean to tell me my beloved baby girl"—*insert eye roll*—"has been interacting with the offspring of some Uncle Tom Republican woman? Do you have any idea of the havoc her policies will wreak on the Black community if she wins this Senate race? What in the world has gotten into you, Shelbi?"

Shelbi had been too stunned to even speak.

Mama (who'd started the whole mess, mind you) then said, "Now hold on, Charles. We don't know anything about the boy."

"Correct," Shelbi said, finding her words then. "You don't. Frankly, there's no need to even consider Andy's mom's politics because he's nothing like her. He's actually pretty great."

"*We* will have to be the judge of *that*, young lady," Daddy said then. "I want to see the Criddle boy at this table for dinner tomorrow night, understand?" (UGH!)

And fine: her parents had been on their best behavior through the meal and even after. But Shelbi doesn't have a clue what she's going to hear once she steps back inside the house.

A knock on her window startles her so bad, Shelbi squeals aloud.

Daddy. (Of course.)

Shelbi rolls the window down.

"Come on in the house, baby girl," he says. "I've got to be at the hospital at four-thirty in the morning for a spinal cord surgery, but I'd like to chat before hittin' the hay."

"I mean, you could totally just go to bed, Daddy. Surely this isn't more important than someone's spine—"

"Girl, if you don't get your tail outta this car and quit playing with me. Family room. Three minutes." And he walks off.

When Shelbi comes in—two and a half minutes later—her parents are waiting for her. Trying to keep her heart rate down, she climbs over the back of her family's massive U-shaped sectional couch and tucks herself tight into one of the cushy corners.

She knows her dread isn't totally unfounded: these "family meetings" typically only occur when she's in trouble. The very first one, she'd just turned fifteen, and Mama had found a bottle of liquid Shelbi wasn't old enough to drink *and* a little baggie of colorful pills that could've gotten her arrested in Shelbi's backpack.

"I swear I haven't done anything illegal," she blurts before either of her parents can speak.

They exchange one of those Mama 'n' Daddy *looks* no child could ever decipher . . . and then both explode into laughter.

"Girl, if you don't relax," Mama says.

"We know you haven't done anything wrong, Shelli Belli," Daddy says. "Quite the opposite, actually . . ."

"We really enjoyed Walter—"

"Andy," Shelbi corrects Mama without thinking. "I mean . . . sorry."

"*Andy* seems like a wonderful young man," Mama continues.

"Helpful that he didn't seem to be trying to get up your dress," Daddy chimes in. "You know a father can tell, now."

"Wow." Shelbi puts her face in her hands.

"Anyway, we just wanted to let you know we approve," Mama says.

At this, Shelbi's head snaps up. "Huh?"

"I'll admit I'm still a tad wary about his mama's ideologies seeping in and poisoning his brain cells—"

"As a neurosurgeon, I'm *sure* you know that's not a thing, Dad?"

Daddy laughs. "You know what I mean. Point being, I'd be lying if I said I'm not nervous about all this. You're my baby girl and I want to keep you safe," he says. "But *our* therapist—your mama's and mine, I mean—has been stressing the importance of trusting *your* judgment."

"And as long as *you* aren't ignoring any red flags"— Mama begins, and Walter's "water" bottle immediately pops into Shelbi's head, but she shoves it aside—"we'll follow your lead here."

"To an *extent*, now. If we notice anything awry with you, it's on and poppin', you hear me?"

Shelbi rolls her eyes and smiles. "Yes, Daddy."

"We hope you enjoy your time with the young man," Mama says. "He's welcome over here whenever—"

"Just not in your *bed*room, understand?"

Shelbi laughs, surprising even herself. It's been a while since she felt this . . . light. Especially while talking to her sometimes-maybe-a-little-overprotective parents. "Of course, Daddy. No boys in my room."

"Now don't get it twisted," Daddy pipes in. "This isn't a decision we arrived at quickly. Your mother and I had some discussions *pre*-dinner about what *we* would perceive as red flags, and we were watchin' your boy very closely from the moment he walked in the house—"

"And he seems like a delightful young man," Mama cuts in while shooting a little glare at Daddy, as though he said more than he was supposed to.

"At any rate: glad we're on the same page." He claps once and stands. "Well, I'm calling it a night. Surgery tomorrow is a doozie. Young man sustained a traumatic brain injury trying to ride his skateboard down a *moving* escalator handrail on a dare." He shakes his head and strolls off, mumbling something about *kids these days* . . .

Shelbi and her mama lock eyes. "You good?" Mama says knowingly. "I'm sure this is a lot to take in, us insisting on meeting this boy, then turning around and more or less giving you free rein with him."

Shelbi couldn't have said it better herself. "It's a little surprising? First the car, and now this? It's a lot of . . . ummm . . ."

"Freedom?"

Yes. "Precisely."

"Well, we love you, and we're proud of you, we believe in you, and we want to prove to you that we trust you and value your autonomy," Mama says. "Also, you're about to go to college, so might as well get this whole independence thing underway, don't you think?"

"But . . ." *What about what happened before? What if I mess up again? What if I make a wrong choice and ruin another life? What if something happens and I wind up having to go back to the hospital? What if—*

"You bring a lot of good into the world, my love." Mama is suddenly right beside Shelbi with her hand on Shelbi's knee.

And before she can think too much about it, Shelbi lunges and wraps her arms around her mama's waist and puts her head on her shoulder. Now she's crying. Whether from gratitude or from fear, she's not entirely sure. Maybe a bit of both.

"Thank you, Mama," Shelbi says. "I won't let you down. Scout's honor."

Hi.

Hey!

Thanks again for coming over.

Are you kidding?

Thank YOU for having me

Is it weird that I *might* be a little bit in love with your parents?

Yes.

It is.

But I'll let you slide this time. Lol.

Your mom is amazing.

She's so like . . . warm. And nurturing. And like . . . full of love.

I mean, gotta be full of SOMETHING to write the filth she does, am I right?

Haha! Touché.

Real talk though: this signed book is officially my most prized possession.

And Shonda Crenshaw literally HANDED me the copy!

She really liked you.

Ah you're just saying that to make me feel like less of a geeky fanboy.

LOL! I'm serious! I got called into a whole family meeting once I got back from dropping you off, but it was literally just my parents letting me know they liked you.

Wait, really?

Really.

In fact, my dad was pleasantly surprised that you're nothing like your mom.

That might be the nicest thing anyone's ever said to me, Shelbi.

Lol!

Side note: I'm pretty sure you've made me laugh more in the past three weeks than anyone has since my diagnosis.

Well, I'm glad my idiocy is amusing to someone.

RELIEF.

In fact, Andy is so glad—and relieved that Shelbi's parents liked him—he doesn't drink for three whole days.

Tacos.

When Walter called about the food truck festival, Shelbi initially thought he was trying to make a move. And she almost said so. His pitch was adorable: *Uhh hey, so my dad was given a couple of tickets to that Westside Food Truck Fest thing that sold out in like the first five minutes, and he offered them to me, so I was wondering if maybe you wanted to go?* But also suspect. *As friends, I mean,* he quickly added.

Shelbi, caught off guard, had responded *Hmm?* and he'd cleared things right on up: *Just saying it wouldn't be a* date *or anything like that.*

So, relieved (though also maybe a teensy bit disappointed—not that she would ever say that aloud), she agreed. To going—as friends—on a not-date with Walter.

Yet the day of, she finds herself fretting over . . . just about everything. What to wear, how to style her hair, does she wear perfume or would that be overkill, are her toenails the right color for open-toed shoes, which ear-rings, what *other* jewelry (if any), etc. etc. etc.

It's ridiculous.

The other thing strumming at her nerves like they're un-tuned guitar strings: after Shelbi said yes to Walter, she im-mediately hung up and called Becky . . . who screeched in Shelbi's ear because she'll be at the food truck festival too.

Which means Shelbi will not only be *out* with Walter on their first one-on-one, non-volunteer-nor-exercise ex-cursion since deciding to be friends, she'll also be intro-ducing him to the only other person their age she has a healthy relationship with. And Becky is *sure* to comment on Shelbi's appearance in some way or another, so Shelbi *has* to be cute.

The pressure is real.

Shelbi settles on a black-and-cream ikat-print midi dress with Air Jordan 1s, and she wraps her hair up in a matching head scarf.

But then she can't bring herself to drive. (*What if there's no parking anywhere? What if she tries to parallel park on some random street and clips someone else's car? What if someone hits her parked car? What if someone steals her car?*)

By the time she and Mario are pulling up in front of the Criddle home, Shelbi is on the brink of a tried-and-true panic attack. And she feels *quite* ridiculous about it considering this Isn't. A. Date. (UGH!)

At least it's not *supposed* to be. Once Walter's in the car, though, the whole ride over is tense. And it's not all on Shelbi: if Walter's bouncing knee is any indication, he's just as nervous as she is.

The tension sticks—well, thickens really—once they're out of the car. When Walter finally *sees* Shelbi fully, his eyes just about *pop* out of his skull. He tries to hide it, but the lifted brows, intensive blinking, and bobbing Adam's apple are pretty telling.

"You, umm . . ." Bouncy bounce goes that little throat bump of his as he speaks. "You look really nice."

"Oh." Shelbi looks down (like she's forgotten what she's wearing?). "Thank you—"

"BAY-BAAAAY!" Shelbi barely has time to turn before she's practically tackled from the side by a dark-skinned girl a couple inches shorter than her with wide hips and box braids that go down to her butt. "Oh mai Gaaaaahd! UGH, I missed you so much!"

Becky. Squeezing the life out of Shelbi now.

"You scared the crap out of me, I just want you to know," Shelbi says to her cousin. "Also definitely cutting off the circulation to my lower extremities."

"Oh, whatever, you'll be aiight." (Though she does let go.) "OMG, is this the infamous *Walter*? Girl, why you ain't tell he was *fine* fine?!"

"Beck, you don't even *like* boys."

"Okay, and? Don't mean I can't see when a dude is

attractive." Becky rolls her eyes and then waves flirta-tiously at Walter.

"Ignore her," Shelbi says to him. And then back to Becky: "Aren't you supposed to be on a date or something?"

Becky sucks her teeth. "Child, somebody bumped into her and scuffed her li'l Off-White sneaker or something." Becky waves as though it's the dumbest thing she's ever heard. "Why somebody would pay seven hundred dollars for . . . anyway. Can you let me meet Walter now?"

"You can't call him that," Shelbi says. "He's Andy to you."

Becky rolls her eyes again. "She known him for like a month and already actin' like she *owns* him," she says under her breath. "Hi, *Andy*," she adds, and she extends a hand to Walter. Who has clearly been laughing the whole time. "I don't know what you even *see* in my wack-ass cousin, but it's nice to meet you. I'm Becky."

"Wait." Walter's face morphs into one of confusion, and for a second, Shelbi gets nervous. "What'd you say your name is?"

"Becky Denise Crenshaw-Davis," Becky says with a proud grin.

"How do you spell your first name?"

She lifts an eyebrow (and so does Shelbi). "*B-E-C-K-Y* . . . ?"

"Is it short for something?"

"No . . . why?"

Walter looks at Shelbi, and then back at Becky. Becky, who is now looking at *Shelbi* like *What is wrong with this fool?*

Shelbi speaks up. "Walter, this is my cousin. I mentioned her, remember?"

And this is when Walter opens his mouth and sticks his giant boating shoe inside (has homie ever even *been* on a boat is the real question): "Sorry," he says. "It's really great to meet you . . . It's just that when Shelbi mentioned her cousin Beck, I thought . . . Well, I dunno what I thought, but Becky is the whitest white girl name in the book, so I'm a little taken aback that *that's* what Beck is short for."

And now the only thing Shelbi hears is the sizzling of something in the taco truck behind them because everyone has gone silent.

Becky points at Walter, looks at Shelbi, and says, "Did he just . . . ?"

Shelbi shrugs. "Sounds to me like he did."

(Of note: it's not that Shelbi's *trying* to throw Walter under the bus, but hey: dolls before balls.)

Becky gives Walter the type of once-over that would make the average guy ready to fight, and she grins. "At least nobody would see *my* name and expect somebody's grandpa, *Walter.*"

Shelbi can't help it: she snorts.

"Oh, so you think this is funny?" Walter says, turning to her.

"Whoa now, don't get fresh with *my* cousin," Becky says. "Not if you know what's good for you."

He looks back and forth between the two girls. "Are you . . . What is this, a double-team?"

Neither girl responds (and not that she'd say so because

she wouldn't want to jinx it, but Shelbi is having the time of her life).

"Can I at least buy you both tacos?" he continues. "Like, fine if you want to co-maim me or whatever, but we could at least eat first?"

"Oh, he might be a keeper, Shelbi," Becky says, and then to Walter, "Make it two, and I'll forgive you."

"How 'bout three?" from Walter.

Becky turns to Shelbi with both eyebrows raised. "Oop! Yeah, girl. Wife this one on up and give him some babies."

"Becky, Walter and I are just *friends*."

"Hmph," Becky grunts. "You sure *he* agrees with you on that one?"

Slight spike of panic, but Shelbi stuffs it down. "Yes, I am," she says. "Right, Walter?"

And though it takes him a *bit* longer to answer than Shelbi feels is entirely necessary, *and* he opens with an "Uhhh," he does eventually get the words out. "She's right," he says. "I do agree. Shelbi and I are just friends."

Shelbi ignores the slight pinch in her heart. "See?" she replies. "Just friends."

JUNK.

Four flowers, one barrel. These are the words dancing around in Andy's head as he stares at the bottle of bourbon he popped open this evening. And he really does mean *popped*. This one, unlike the cheap stuff he usually drinks, had a cork in the top. Which he's pretty sure means it was expensive. Though, for the life of him, he can't remember where he got it from.

He's on his second pour.

Three days ago, Andy had one of the best nights he's had . . . maybe ever. Yes, things were . . . tense. Between him and Shelbi. They had been from the moment he got in the car. Well, really even from the moment he'd asked her to go with him. But when he got in the car, and he caught a glimpse of her and got smacked with a whiff of her perfume (*When did she start wearing perfume?!*), Andy knew the evening was going to be interesting.

And it *did* feel like a date that everyone was trying to pretend wasn't a date. Actually, it felt like a *double* date. Despite Becky's apparent annoyance with her (missing) date at the beginning, once the other girl, Trish, came back, it was *very* clear that she and Becky were super into each other. Andy has no doubt that their effusive PDA contributed to the weird, electric-ish thing zipping around and between him and his (gorgeous) *not*-date.

Becky did eventually explain that her mom, Sharmaine— Shelbi's mom's *other* sister, who is older by a year—named her Becky *as a means of Trojan horsing the magic of Black femininity into spaces that would reject a name for sounding "too black."* "Let's not forget," Becky said, "I was born pre-Obama. Wasn't no movements pointing out racism in oh-five."

The whole birth year thing is how Andy discovered that Shelbi and Becky are the same age, but Shelbi skipped a grade and will be sixteen for another few weeks. ("Don't catch a case dealing with this *child*," Becky said upon hearing that Andy is eighteen.) Which is how Andy discovered that . . . he's maybe more into Shelbi than he wants to acknowledge.

However, none of that is what pushed him to grab this bottle of clearly not-cheap whiskey today . . . while the sun is very much still up. Yeah, he was a little down and wanted to talk to her (though he also didn't want to seem too eager, so he didn't reach out). And yes, he misses Shelbi far more than he wants to. But the shove into *Screw it, I'm having a drink* territory came at the hands of one Cristine R. Criddle.

Andy and Dad had been at the kitchen table just . . . sitting. Like they did sometimes. Dad reading a newspaper, Andy inhaling a rather large bowl of sugary cereal. A peaceful Criddle-Man late afternoon. But then Mom came barreling into the kitchen looking like she'd just learned of an opponent's plot to steal the Senate election, and out of nowhere goes: "We need to turn that fifth bedroom into a guest space. It's time."

Dad and Andy had looked at each other like *Huh?* And then Dad said, "Fifth bedroom?" at the exact moment it clicked for Andy: she was talking about Emma's room.

"Yes, the fifth bedroom," she replied. "The one currently filled with Emma's junk—"

"Emma's *what* now?" Andy said.

Congresswoman Cris had drawn back in surprise. So, Andy said what was on his mind: "What kind of mother calls their dead three-year-old's stuff *junk* and decides to more or less erase her memory from a home?"

"*Excuse* me?" she said then. "Last I check, *I* pay for this—"

"*We*," Dad cut in. "*We* pay for this house. You *and* I. And Andy's right. Emma's stuff isn't *junk*, Cristine. How could you even say that?"

"Great, so now *I'm* the bad guy for wanting to make use of an unused space—"

"You're the 'bad guy' because the only person you care about is yourself," Andy said, getting up from his chair. "Oh, and your *constituents*. We know you care a whole heck of a lot about them." And he left the kitchen.

Once back in his room, Andy had paced. Back and forth, back and forth. Part of him wanted to leave . . . but he didn't really have anywhere to go. Also, who knew what constituents might see him angrily walking down the street (he still had neither car nor license). He was also feeling protective of Emma's space and felt he needed to stick around just to make sure Monster Mom didn't defile it in any way.

He'd dropped down onto his couch, fuming and pondering—always a terrible combination for Andy. He obviously wanted to call Shelbi, but thinking of her made him think of *her* parents. How happy and in love they seemed. Which made him think about Stephanie. He thought he'd been in love with her before everything went south . . . but what if he was wrong? Being around Shelbi makes him feel like maybe he *was* wrong, but he's not actually *allowed* to be in love with *her*, so . . .

When and how did life get so trash? he thought. And then he was up and headed to his dresser—which he had to move aside to access the little nook in the wall—pulling a bottle from the four left in his secret stash. How fitting that the type he grabbed is called Four Roses. Also kind of nice that it doesn't smell or taste like gasoline.

He really wants to call Shelbi. Like really bad. Even just to hear her voice. The backs of their hands brushed a few times during their quest to find the shaved-ice truck, and this little zing of something would creep up Andy's arm like a handful of spiders beneath his skin. It was awesome.

There was also this one time when Trish had gone to get something called monkey bread from a truck selling Hawaiian food, and Shelbi accidentally backed into Andy while arguing with Becky about hair products or something. And she'd said she was sorry . . . but then she didn't move away. So there was, like, *maybe* an inch of space between her lovely backside (not that Andy *noticed* how lovely it looked in her dress or anything . . .) and his front side. He's a full head and some change taller, so it's not like his view was obscured or anything—he could see right over the top of her. But with her that close, he could smell her over the smorgasbord of food fragrances. And man . . . it was kind of a lot.

Up until then, he'd managed to keep his thoughts *mostly* friendly. But right now? With him feeling the way he does? All alone and sad and pissed and hating his mom, but also hating himself and wanting to talk to his friend, however knowing deep down that he wants to be more than *her* friend, and soon his sister's room might not be her room anymore even though it hasn't really *been* her room in months because *she's* not here anymore, and what about her baby doll? Mom couldn't possibly think Baby (that's what Emma called the doll) is *junk* considering she was Emma's most prized possession and . . . Jesus, is his cup empty *again*?

He reaches for the bottle, but before he can grab it, his phone buzzes in his pocket.

> Hey, any chance you could come over?

> I could really use a friend.

Well, *that's* a no-brainer.

> Of course.

> Just be forewarned: I'm a little tipsy.

(Because he had to tell her, right? Showing up like this with no warning certainly doesn't seem like the thing to do. But neither does not showing up at all. Hopefully the honesty doesn't backfire . . .)

> You want me to send Mario to get you?

> He literally knocked on my door five minutes ago, asking if I needed to go anywhere because he's bored.

> Nah, I'll walk across the field.

> I'm sure the air and exercise will do me some good.

Swim.

Shelbi sips rooibos tea by the pool as she waits. Vaguely jealous that Walter is tipsy.

She pulls her hand away from her phone. In truth, she'd like to shoot him another text, asking him to bring her some of whatever he's been drinking. Even if it's that propane-smelling junk she emptied from his water bottle.

There's no alcohol inside her house (that whole *Would you like a scotch?* stunt Daddy pulled really was a "test," as he put it), and for good reason. But if there was ever a time she'd *want* to have a drink, this is it. Would she wind up wanting to crawl beneath her bed and go to sleep forever twenty-four hours from now? Absolutely. Alcohol *is* a depressant, after all, and she's already learned the hard way that, for her, depressant cancels out *anti*depressant and leads to intensified depression (*so* much fun, let her tell you).

But still. Right now? Man, it would be great to just intoxicate herself away from it all.

The folding glass door opens behind her, and she instinctively turns.

There he is.

And then she's up and rushing over to wrap her arms around his waist and bury her face in his chest. He smells like bourbon. (And yes: Shelbi Camille Augustine *absolutely* knows what bourbon smells like.) She breathes a sigh of relief that Daddy's in surgery and therefore *not* here to greet Walter. Because he also absolutely knows what bourbon smells like. That would've been a disaster.

"Thank you for coming," she says.

But he doesn't respond.

In fact, his arms are just hanging at his sides, and he's

made no move to hug Shelbi back. Which is weird. "Wal-ter?" she says, pulling away to look up at his face.

He's staring at the pool, looking like he's seen some earthbound spirit—

Oh no.

"Oh my God, I'm so sorry," Shelbi says, instantly furious with herself for being so careless. *Really, Shelbi? You had him brought out to the* pool? *As in a thing that surely reminds him of the instrument of death that took his baby sister? What the hell is even* wrong *with you—*

"I wasn't thinking," she says aloud, cutting off the negative thoughts before they can consume her. (Took her *years* to learn how to do that.) "Let's go inside. I . . . ugh." And she smacks her forehead a few times.

Which apparently gets *his* attention. "Hey, whoa," he says, gently catching her wrist and pulling her hand away from her face.

"You totally hate me now . . . ," Shelbi says, unable to stop herself. "I brought you out to this stupid pool and now you hate me." And *she* hates that he's seeing her this way. Reaching out to him was totally a mistake.

"Don't say that, Shelbi." Now he takes her other hand and looks her right in the eye. "Of course I don't hate you."

"You don't? You're not mad at me?" (*Why does she sound so* pitiful?) "I didn't mean to—I'm so sorry. Too much in my head."

"Don't worry about it. It's fine. I would've had to face a pool again eventually." *Now* he pulls her forward and wraps her arms back around his waist before winding his around her neck and shoulders. "It's honestly probably a good thing I'm with *you* the first time."

And that's it. Shelbi bursts into sobs.

As she stands there, wailing like an infant with her tears soaking through Walter's polo, she can't help but wonder what's going through his mind. But then he squeezes her tighter and he rubs her back. It might be the most soothing thing she's ever experienced. He's strong and solid and he smells nice—in spite of the bourbon.

So Shelbi breathes in deep and exhales. The tension goes out of her shoulders, and she just . . . relaxes.

Which is when he kisses her forehead.

"That better have been a *friendly* kiss, Walter," she mumbles from within the folds of his shirt.

And now he's laughing. "Are you serious right now?" He lets her go and wipes the tears off her cheeks with his thumbs. "You're worried about my forehead peck motivations as you cry and snot and drool all over my good shirt?"

She laughs. And there's the light.

Thank God.

"Can we sit?" she asks. "It can totally be inside if you prefer."

"Nah, we're good out here," he replies. "The fresh air is nice."

He pulls one of the pool chairs right up next to the one

Shelbi returns to, and they both sit all the way back with their feet up.

"What happened?" Shelbi says.

"Huh?"

"You're tipsy at five p.m. on a Wednesday. Something must have happened."

"Umm, aren't we here to talk about you? I'm not the one who sent the SOS."

Deflection attempt: Failed.

"So?" he continues. "What's going on with *you?*"

Shelbi takes another deep breath. In truth, she hadn't really been thinking clearly when she reached out. She was just . . . panicked. And Walter was the first person who came to mind.

Shelbi peeks over at him. He's staring at her with his hands clasped in his lap. Waiting. With a giant wet spot on his shirt that *she* put there with her tears.

Why is being vulnerable so uncomfortable?

"Okay, so you remember how I told you the last 'friend' I had did a very unfriendly thing?"

"Sure do. I think it'd be impossible for me to forget considering the vendetta I now have against this mystery person."

"Well, she's dead, so you can let it go."

He doesn't respond to that.

"Sorry, that was kind of a harsh way to put it."

"I mean . . . if it's true, it's true, right?"

Now she can't help but smile at him. "Couldn't have said it better myself," she says. "I'm really glad you're my friend."

"Uhhh . . . you're welcome, I guess?"

"I'll spare you the ugly details, her name included, because I don't think any of it is pertinent to the story. But the broad strokes: After I changed schools for the first time back in California, I made this . . . friend. She was cute and funny and exciting to be around most of the time, but the more I got to know her, the more I realized she had this nasty mean streak where she would do and say awful things to people seemingly for no reason at all."

"Okay," Walter says. "I'm tracking."

"Well, being a naïve fifteen-year-old who was still getting used to my diagnosis and medications, on *top* of being at a new school, I kind of ignored it. She was never directly mean to *me*, so like . . . whatever, no big deal, right?"

"I'm guessing the correct answer is *wrong*?"

Shelbi laughs. She *really* likes this guy. Which is vaguely terrifying.

Anyway:

"*Wrong* is correct," she says. "As I mentioned, when the season changed, I experienced my first mixed episode. Not sure if you decided to look it up, but *my* experience of it was like . . . having the super-negative thoughts and outlook and heaviness of depression, but with, like, intensely high energy levels. So I was incredibly sad and detached and withdrawn and feeling like there was no point in living. But I also couldn't sleep. And my thoughts would race. And I would have these bursts where I couldn't stop talking. And when I wanted to accomplish something, it had to be done like *right then*."

"That sounds terrible, Shelbi."

"Definitely not a time I look back on with fondness. Anyway, while I'm going through all that, this girl flips into one of her mean streaks. This time with *me* as the target. For the first week and a half, I didn't really know what was going on with me, and I was taking my meds and stuff like I was supposed to, so she and I just chalked it up to me still adjusting to the new school."

"Okay . . ."

"But there was this one night when all of my racing thoughts involved doing awful things to myself. And I called my 'friend' thinking . . . well, I'm not sure *what* I was thinking, but I opened up and told her about the stuff going through my head, and she basically encouraged me to 'go with' what my mind was 'showing' me and off myself."

"Wait . . . *What?*"

"Right. Again: not getting into the details." Shelbi forces herself to continue—honestly, a year and a half later, she's still a bit in disbelief—"But let's just say she used a slur or two from that list and agreed that the world would be better without people like me in it."

Walter is quiet for a beat, and then: "I don't even know what to say to that."

"The worst part is that I almost believed her, Walter. I kinda had a thing for her at that point, so the romantic feelings really messed with my thinking. Over the next week, she bombarded me with really mean text messages—that I subsequently deleted, so I wound up with no proof. But most of the scars on my side happened over the course of the eight days she was tormenting me. I'm pretty sure it only stopped because I . . . well, I pressed down a little *too* hard one night and wound up having to go to the hospital because I needed stitches. Told my parents everything, and they immediately pulled me out of school and changed my phone number and all that."

"And you eventually wound up here."

"Correct."

They lapse into silence for a minute. And it's comfortable. Which is nice. Then Walter says: "So how'd she die?"

"Suspected suicide."

"Really?!"

"Mmhmm. She was likely dealing with something undiagnosed. Her dad was a lot like my granny when it came to questions of mental health."

"Man."

"I'm really sad about it," Shelbi says then. "Even though she wound up being awful to me, I hate knowing that *she* was probably suffering."

Walter shakes his head. "You might be the kindest person I know, Shelbi."

"I went on her Instagram, and a bunch of people have

posted some really messed-up comments beneath her final post. And I know I shouldn't have done that . . . like for my *own* good. But I just like . . . man, I wish more people would take the time to *consider* what it might be like to live with a brain that works like mine. To have your own mind tell you you're not worth the air you breathe. Do you have any idea what it's like to feel like you're the queen of the universe one minute, and a waste of molecules the next?"

"No," Walter says. "I don't."

"That was totally rhetorical, but thank you for acknowledging it."

Now Walter laughs. Which makes Shelbi laugh.

And just like that, she feels much better.

"I'm really sorry, Shelbi," Walter says.

"None of this is your fault, Wal-Wal. I appreciate you being here, but I'm also sorry you have to see me like this."

"Hey now, let's not forget number seven in our agreement . . . no holds barred, right?" He reaches over and gently shoves her shoulder.

Shelbi swings her legs over the side of her pool chair and sits up to face Walter. He's gazing at the water. "What's going through your mind?"

"Hmm?"

"Being . . ."—she gestures to the pool—"near that."

His eyes narrow, but just for a moment. "Well, it's not as hard as I thought it'd be," he says. "Though that's probably because you're here with me."

"Oh, whatever."

Walter turns and looks over Shelbi's face in a way that make it very warm, then his eyes narrow, and he says, "Come," as he stands and pulls her to her feet.

"Where are we go— OH!" she says as Walter scoops her up into his arms. He walks to the edge of the pool.

"Shelbi," he says, "unexpected things happen, but know that as long as I'm able, I'll be here for you."

Before she can figure out what the heck he's talking about, he throws her in.

And as Shelbi surfaces, soaked and screaming and cussing about her hair (the *nerve!*), Walter removes his shirt and shoes.

And he dives in after her.

So.

Actually, wait, before I get into that, I will have you know that . . .

I still hate you.

Hahahaha!

Awww come on, little fishy!

That was like two and a half whole days ago, and I've totally had a lovely dinner with you and your awesome parents again since!

Whatever.

My hair is never going to forgive you.

Well that's unfortunate.

But clearly not the reason you're texting me.

Hush.

I'm right though, aren't I?

Yes.

But don't let it go to your head.

The real reason I reached out is because my family, Becky and Bibi included, is going down to Florida for a cousin's wedding next week.

That sounds absolutely delightful.

If your question is "Will Walter miss me while I'm gone?" the answer is a resounding yes.

Actually, my question is "Would Walter like to join us?"

Huh?

It's technically not even MY question.

It's my parents' question.

This morning, when Dr. Charles Augustine dropped the news that we're going, HE said, "Your mother and I discussed it and we think you should invite your friend Walter."

And let me guess: you corrected them to "Andy."

Yes I did, but that is neither here nor there.

Now that you know the background, I will present the question again: Walter, would you like to come to Florida for a few days with me and my family?

I mean . . . This just feels so sudden.

Tell me about it. You're just as shocked as I was.

Are you planning to propose while we're there?

Like do I need to pack my linen mack-daddy short set?

Nobody says "mack daddy" anymore.

Guess I'll take that as a no . . .

Oh my God, will you just answer?

Is the anticipation killing you, Shelbi Augustine?

YES!

Well that's my answer. Pending parental approval.

Huh?

My answer is yes, Shelbi. I'd be delighted to accompany you.

See, now was that so difficult?

Of course not. I just enjoy giving you a hard time.

Well now we're just back to where we started.

As I said at the start of this conversation: I hate you.

Yeah yeah yeah. Sure you do.

(Aside.

The moment Shelbi puts her phone down, she has to run downstairs and get an ice pack for her chest. It's one of the few things that calm her when she's on the verge of an anxiety spiral—which frequently leads to a panic attack.

The truth: She didn't really *want* to invite Walter. For a number of reasons. Like: She shared a *lot* with him by the pool a few days ago and still feels weird about telling him so much. Also, she really *is* trying to keep from catching feelings. *And* she's never been around him at night . . . which seems to be when he drinks. Not that there would be any alcohol on the trip.

Anyway, Mama and Daddy were quite enthusiastic about the invite—she overheard Daddy say something about Wal seeming "to inspire such positive affect in baby girl's moods" and potentially being "quite the delightful accompaniment." She couldn't tell her parents *she* was wary because then they would start bugging out and wondering why. So here she is.

He's going to see her in a bathing suit. And they'll be around each other for *days.*

Hopefully this isn't a total disaster.)

ROAD TRIP.

DAY 1:

At 6:55 a.m., a dark-green Chevrolet Suburban pulls up in front of Andy's house. A beautiful, older Indian woman— Shelbi's bibi, he presumes—waves at him from the passenger seat. And then Dr. Augustine gets out to greet Andy's dad and grab Andy's bag to put it in the trunk. After acknowledging everyone, Andy climbs into the rearmost seat next to Shelbi, who smiles like she's seeing the sun after weeks of rain. (Andy's smile is no less intense, mind you.)

"Everyone buckled?" Dr. Augustine rumbles as he gets back in.

There's a collective "Yes!"

"Wonderful. Estimated drive time is five hours and thirty-one minutes plus stops. Let's ride!"

Two TV screens flip down from the ceiling. As the first Tom-Holland-as-Spider-Man movie comes on, Shelbi touches Andy's hand: "This is a rental, by the way," she says. And he laughs.

The drive down is nice, barring a very awkward forty-five-minute stretch where they pass cotton field after cotton field in South Alabama. The awkwardness is really Shelbi's fault because as the first one comes into view, she says, "Daddy, what's the temperature outside?"

"Approaching eighty-six degrees Fahrenheit, baby girl," he responds.

"God," she says. "And it's barely ten a.m. here. Can you imagine what enslaved people went through working those fields in the middle of the day?"

And despite the fact that Andy was literally thinking the same thing, when she turns to look at him, she says, "Oh, wait, you're mixed and light-skinned, so you probably would've been in the house."

Becky and Shonda both start laughing hysterically, and Dr. Augustine says, "Damn, Shelli Belli. Cut the kid some slack." Which is when Shelbi's eyes go horrified-humongous, and she says, "Oh God, I totally didn't mean it like that, Wal-Wal! I'm so sorry!"

Everyone laughs (Bibi included), and the tension breaks, but every time they pass a field after that, this loaded silence settles down in the car like everyone is holding their breath.

The Suburban pulls into the driveway of the rented house on Carillon Beach at 12:08 p.m. Central Time, and everyone gets unloaded and settled in. The day passes quickly, there's a crab boil for dinner, and then around the lit fire pit on the house's back deck, s'mores are made and scary stories exchanged—during which Shelbi scoots closer and closer to Andy until she's practically under his arm.

It's the best night he's had in as long as he can remember.

DAY 2:

Shelbi insisted that Andy go to bed at 10:00 p.m. last night, and now he knows why: at 5:35 a.m., wearing yoga pants and a tank top, she busts into his room and tries to drag him out of bed. He fights tooth and nail because, hello, it's *morning* and he's a *dude*. Some wholly natural biological occurrences are better left unseen.

Within ten minutes, however, Andy and Shelbi are standing on the beach (has it been mentioned that stepping off the back porch of their rather large vacation dwelling involves stepping right into the sand?). They begin a strenuous piloga session as the sun rises.

By the time they head back inside, both sweaty and endorphin-fueled and ready to dive right into the day, Bibi has made a beverage Shelbi calls *kaapi*, which she says is coffee blended with something called chicory. Shelbi doesn't drink any because caffeine is a apparently a no-no for her, but when Bibi offers Andy a cup, he takes it.

And he's glad. Because it's delicious.

As he sips, Andy watches Shelbi pour Grape-Nuts into a bowl and then add a handful of what look like Lucky Charms marshmallows pulled from a ziplock bag. Then she pours a pale-brown liquid over the top and begins to eat.

Andy is confused. "Did you just mix Lucky's marshmallows with *Grape-Nuts*?" he asks. "And what the heck is that brown stuff?"

"Brown stuff is flax milk," Shelbi replies. "Bibi makes it for me, and it's brown so I won't ever confuse it with baby cow food and accidentally die."

"I . . . *What?*"

"Ya girl is allergic to dairy, Grandpa," Becky says as she steps into the kitchen. She's still got her bonnet on, which makes her pretty adorable even though she's clearly real ornery even first thing in the morning.

"Yup." Shelbi puts another spoonful of cereal in her mouth.

Andy shakes his head. "Okay, I get the flax milk, but that cereal blend is . . . how do you even eat that, Shelbi? It's the equivalent of throwing a cup of sugar on some wood chips."

"Hey, this cereal blend is a metaphor for *life*. You get your sweet, enjoyable bits and your unsweet, awful bits in the same bowl. Gotta take the good with the bad, Wal-Wal. Here, taste . . ." She holds her cereal-filled spoon out.

Andy reluctantly opens his mouth and . . . well, she's got a point. Flax milk aside—no shade to Bibi, but that junk is *nasty*—the two cereal elements do balance each other out.

"Interesting," Andy says, and she laughs. Andy finds himself wanting to kiss her dimples, but he can't because they're just friends.

Sweet bits and unsweet bits in the same bowl, indeed.

Once everyone is awake and has eaten, the ladies sequester themselves in Bibi's bedroom to get ready for the wedding they all came to attend. Dr. Augustine tells Andy that Bibi's sister's grandson will be joined to his Nigerian American college sweetheart in a lavish, multitraditional ceremony.

Apparently getting a sari properly wrapped and draped— Bibi, Becky, Shonda, and Shelbi will all be wearing them— is a very intricate and time-consuming process. As a matter of fact, Andy and Dr. Augustine begin the quarter-mile walk down to the section of beach where the wedding will take place before the ladies even come out. (And it *might* be said that the whole not-seeing-Shelbi-before-the-wedding thing leads Andy's imagination to places it shouldn't go.)

Wedding attendees trickle in, literally *all* of them in brightly colored saris and scarves and tunics and dashikis and kente-print dresses and skirts and head wraps. Soon the beach looks like it's been scattered with a bag of potpourri. Andy's favorite part: everyone's barefoot.

He's absorbing the epicness of the scene when he hears Shelbi's lyrical laughter and his head turns . . .

And now he can't breathe because she looks too amazing.

Her sari is the color of the ocean (how appropriate), with a silver pattern stitched across the lower edge, and he can see the peek of her brown skin at her waist. Her glasses are gone, and she has a red dot between her eyebrows like Bibi does, except hers has something sparkly in the center.

A gust of wind comes off the water and catches in her hair as she heads in Andy's direction. So with the sari billowing and the hair blowing and the smile gleaming as they lock eyes, Andy feels like he's in a cheesy romantic comedy. It makes him want to do cheesy romantic comedy things like meet her halfway and sweep her up into one of those spin-around hugs and tell her how the world stopped when she stepped onto the beach because she looks like a goddess.

But he resists. "Nice dot," he says instead, and she laughs. "Bindi," she says. "It's called a bindi."

And then she wraps her arms around his waist and squeezes tight.

He wonders if she can feel how fast his heart is beating.

Stars.

NIGHT 2/DAY 3:

Shelbi can't stop thinking about how fast Walter's heart was beating. She's lying in bed, staring up at the ceiling and trying her hardest not to wonder what he might be doing at the other end of the house.

The night was like nothing she'd ever experienced. The colors and the music and the dancing . . . she had no idea Walter could move the way he did. Homeboy held everyone in *thrall* on that reception dance floor, and the wedding was totally dry—not a drop of alcohol in sight—so it was all him. She'd also be lying if she said she didn't thoroughly enjoy the closeness when he was dancing with her. Bibi clearly liked seeing Shelbi and Walter dancing together too, considering the way she kept winking and grinning. (So grandma-typical.)

At some point she must have dozed off, because the next thing *she* knows, there's a tap on her shoulder, and when she opens her eyes, sunlight is streaming through the window of the bedroom she's sharing with Becky. Walter is standing over her with a yoga mat tucked under his arm. "Get your act together, slacker," he says.

Piloga, breakfast, then beach. And *man*, does Walter Andrew Criddle look scrumptious without a shirt on. She'd averted her eyes during his little pool stunt, but there's no looking away this morning.

Backfires, though. By early afternoon, he's red as a fire truck.

Which means all of his windsurfing, Jet Skiing, fun-in-the-sunning plans for the afternoon have alit on his stinging skin and burst into flames. The guy can't even *put* a shirt on.

And of course, Shelbi can't leave *her* guest behind at the house while everyone else goes out to have fun. So Becky, Mama, Daddy, and Bibi carry on with their plans, but she spends the day indoors, laughing and talking and watching the latest superhero movies with the boy of the best-friend dreams she didn't know she had.

She definitely makes it a point to poke fun at good ol' Walty-Wal-Wal for his lack of melanin and "susceptibility to UV Kryptonite" while they're watching *Man of Steel*, but she's also the person who cuts leaves from the aloe vera plant in the foyer of the beach house ("It's like the owners knew this would be useful," she says) and rubs his back and shoulders with the gel.

Since it's their last day in this particular iteration of paradise, once the sun's been down for a while, Shelbi convinces Walter to take a walk on the beach. Who knows how far they go, but soon they've stopped to just gaze up at a dark sky that looks like it's been doused with glitter.

It's impossible to find the moon because it's fully in the new phase, but Shelbi does point out Polaris and Arcturus and a dot she knows is Mars and another she knows is Saturn. Walter seems fascinated, so she continues to move through conglomerations of stars—Ursas Major and Minor, and Leo and Scorpio and Boötes.

Their fingers brush and they go silent. So Shelbi turns her palm up. Walter slips his hand into hers, and their fingers fit together like puzzle pieces. The sky sparkles above their heads as the waves crash near their feet, and as corny as it would sound were she to say it aloud, Shelbi knows for a fact that this is the closest to natural bliss she's ever been.

REGRESSION.

For the life of him, Andy can't figure out what he did wrong.

It's been four days since he returned from the beach

trip that he's *sure* flipped his entire world over. And the drive home was the best part: Shelbi spent the bulk of it lying across the backseat with her head on his thigh, just sleeping away. Knowing she felt *safe* enough with him to do that? Especially considering all the stuff she's been through? By the time Dr. Augustine pulled into the Criddles' driveway, Andy felt like he could easily pick up Mount Kilimanjaro and hurl it into the Arabian Sea.

Unfortunately, watching Shelbi wave to him as they pulled off was the last time he felt anything remotely positive because she hasn't spoken to him much since. And it's not like *he* hasn't tried to initiate. She's just . . . gone cold.

Andy wonders if it's because she can tell he has officially broken rule six. When she didn't answer his text message for *three hours* not too long after they got back, he nibbled three of his fingernails down to the skin, something he hadn't done since ninth grade.

He had to admit it to himself then: he, Walter Andrew Criddle, is totally in love with Shelbi Camille Augustine.

Maybe she could sense it in the messages he sent—even though he *thought* they were pretty neutral. Or maybe . . .

He has no idea.

He tries to lose himself in a book—*Swirl*, the final volume in Shonda's White Gangsta series—but that definitely backfires. Tay-Tay and Connor *do* wind up together: At the beginning of the book, they go back to the place they first met, and he proposes. (Andy doesn't think this is very romantic because it's outside what wound up being a crack house, but what does *he* know?) Tay-Tay says yes, of course, but unfortunately, they find out their daughter has some uncurable disease shortly thereafter. Quantavious gets sentenced to life in prison (thank *God*) but not until he wrecks a bunch of people's lives, including that of his side piece, Mercedes, who always wanted a baby, but . . .

Yeah, he doesn't even want to get into it because he'll 100 percent fall apart.

> Hey Shelbi, I just finished the White Gangsta series, and it was uhhh . . . a lot. .

> Definitely reminded me of your Grape-Nuts with marshmallows metaphor.

After about thirty seconds, the word read pops up beneath Andy's messages . . . but then he waits five more, and she doesn't respond. So he tosses his phone across the room onto his couch and stares out his window.

Not even a minute later, a clump of dark clouds pushes its way in front of the sun, and despite being very antisuperstitious, Andy gets a literal chill: it feels like a bad omen.

A car door slams outside, and the feeling intensifies.

(One of the benefits/drawbacks of having a bedroom on the first floor is that he can hear freaking everything going on outside.) Then the front door opens and shuts, and his mom's laughter rings through the air . . . something he hasn't heard in literally over a year.

Andy's got little bullets of sweat exiting the pores at his hairline now, but as curious as he is about the source of her sudden upswing in mood, he decides it's in his own best interests to keep his distance.

But then his mom pokes her head in his room with this mega-smile on her face. "I have a surprise for yoooou," she trills like a drunken songbird.

This is when Andy *knows* everything's about to go to hell.

He gets up. Wipes his face and puts on a shirt. Walks out of his bedroom, down the short hallway, past the kitchen—dread growing with each step (what was he supposed to do, tell Mom he wasn't coming out?)—and into the living room . . .

He stops dead. Because there in front of him . . . is Stephanie.

Being up front: Stephanie is—and has always been—gorgeous. She's mixed like him (also Black mom), tall, slim, honey-blond, stunning green eyes—she's everything Andy thought he was supposed to want in a girlfriend (he can't say the same for *Walter*, but we'll leave that alone for now).

She and Andy met when Mom was first elected to

Congress and on the hunt for "reputable legal counsel to keep on retainer." Mom ended up hiring Stephanie's dad (Jacob Locke, Esq.—aka the guy pictured in the record books next to *World's Biggest D*ckhead*), and Stephanie and Andy eventually started dating despite going to different schools.

Then things went really bad.

Now she's standing here looking just as awkward as Andy feels, and he can't believe Mom would bring her here like this. He certainly can't believe Mr. Locke would agree to a spur-of-the-moment reunion, but there he is, sitting on the couch. Andy is both relieved and furious that Dad's not home—he's 98 percent sure his old man can't stand the guy and that it would be even more uncomfortable if Dad *were* here.

"Well, don't just stand there gaping, Andy!" Mom says. "Say hello!" She's chirping. Like this is a most *delightful* occasion. And maybe it is for her . . . though Andy can't see how it would be, considering—

Never mind. He's not going there.

Andy takes a deep breath and forces a smile. There's still a *ton* of unresolved hurt between him and Steph, but he tries to push past it. "It's good to see you, Steph," he says. "How's it going?"

She smiles, and Andy thinks, *That smile used to put the wind in my sails.* Not so much anymore, though, considering his new dream girl is as different from Steph as night is from day.

"It's going well, Andy," Steph replies, and her voice is just as lilting and twangy as he remembers. "It's good to see you, too."

And that's all. Because really, considering everything, is there anything else for them to say to each other?

"So, Andy," Mr. Locke practically hollers. (Has Andy mentioned how much he hates this bastard?) "What's with this DUI business?"

Andy shrugs. "What can I say, Mr. Locke? As I'm sure you know, shit happens."

"*Language*, Andrew!" Mom looks mortified, and Stephanie is looking at Andy like she's never seen him before.

Mr. Locke doesn't even flinch. "You pled *nolo*, I assume?"

"No offense, sir, but it's really none of your business. You're not even *her* legal counsel anymore." Andy points to the congresswoman. "So you're definitely not mine." (Mom did try to foist Mr. Locke on Andy initially, but he preferred jail to being indebted to that jackhole.)

"All right, boy, don't get your panties in a wad. Just wanted to make sure you were being smart about things. We know your brain hasn't always fired on all cylinders when it comes to difficult situations."

Andy's blood is beginning that proverbial boil, but he keeps his cool. "Well, as one of my favorite book characters says: 'Good lookin' out.'" He's using the phrase sarcastically, but of course Mr. Locke has no clue what he's saying. Andy can almost see the wispy strands of his comb-over lift in the breeze of the reference as it flies over his head.

"Wow, Andy," Stephanie says. "You've really changed. Life must be weird without Emma—"

Annnnd Andy is finished here. "It was nice seeing you, Stephanie, Mr. Locke. You all enjoy your evening." He walks away with Mom calling his name but not daring to chase him. If she happened to come back to her guests without Andy in tow (and she would), she would have to concede defeat. And Congresswoman Cris Criddle would rather pretend she's perfectly fine standing inside a burning house than concede defeat.

He needs to get out of there before he completely loses it.

One final peek at his phone makes it crystal clear that Shelbi is *icing him out*, as the White Gangsta would say. Which leaves Andy with one other option. And it's the one he should never take when he feels like he's feeling right now because it always leads to trouble. Like waking-up-on-random-couches-and/or-getting-DUIs kind of trouble.

But whatever. His sister's dead, his mom's a monster, he was just forced to look his biggest regret in the face, and his dream girl has gone ghost on him. What the hell else does Walter "Andy" Criddle have to lose?

Hey, this is Shelbi's number, right?

This is Marcus Page.

Umm . . . hi?

Sorry, I know it feels super random that I'm texting you and you're probably wondering how I got your number . . .

Yep, that about sums it up.

Well Midas asked me to text you.

There's uhh . . . a bit of an emergency.

Mmmm . . . not to make this even MORE awkward . . .

But who is Midas?

My bad, I mean Andy.

I forgot you wouldn't know him as that.

We always called him Midas cuz he USED to be the golden boy before he became a raging alcoholic.

You said something about an emergency?

Yeah, speaking of raging alcoholic . . .

Midas is REALLY drunk.

I was having a little gathering at my house and he . . . well honestly I don't know HOW the hell much he had to drink, but he locked himself in the bathroom and is refusing to come out unless you come get him.

Wait, what now?

You read that right.

He's definitely been a little off since his sister died, but I've never seen him THIS bad.

Actually, I'M also requesting that you come get him because he's lowkey freaking me the f out.

Hello?

You still there?

Please still be there . . .

What's the address?

Marcus C. Page has shared a dropped pin.

Confession.

It's official: seeing Walter slowly make his way to the Benz on the arm of a buff Salvadorean dude in Superman pajamas, a suit jacket, and a limo driver cap—she told Mario he didn't need the latter two accessories, but he insisted on wearing them anyway—might be the funniest thing Shelbi's ever seen.

That is until "Midas" is actually in the car.

"Magenta," Shelbi says, flicking the (popped) collar of the polo he's wearing. "Real nice, Wal-Wal. Brings out that drunken flush in your cheeks."

"Don't make fun," he replies. "Currently sitting in the eighth circle of hell."

"The fraud circle, huh? Everlasting darkness and physical torture by demons."

"Of *course* you know exactly what's there. You're like . . . the smartest person ever, you know that?"

Shelbi laughs.

"I mean it, Shelbi." He leans his head back and closes his eyes as Mario pulls off. "You're super smart. And I really am a huge fraud so that particular circle—and the punishment therein—is fitting."

"Ah, who needs hell?" Shelbi replies. "I'd say your current physical state is punishment enough. Drink this." She passes him the thermos she brought. "Sorry I couldn't come *in* to get you, by the way. Party settings trigger a number of memories and behaviors I prefer to keep suppressed when I'm in my right mind."

Walter unscrews the top, takes a sip of what's inside . . . and gags. "Jesus, Mary, Joseph, *and* Abraham, what the hell is this?"

Shelbi laughs again. "It's a concoction I used to make for myself and keep in the fridge to drink when I needed to appear less inebriated and wanted to avoid a hangover," she says. "Orange juice for vitamin C, coconut water for hydration and electrolytes, and ginseng for . . . actually, I don't know what the ginseng is for, but whatever. It won't make you less drunk, but it'll take the edge off and keep you from getting dehydrated."

Walter frowns at the thermos like it just kicked him in the shin unprovoked, and Shelbi laughs . . . again. (Is it terrible that she's *enjoying* this version of him?) "Just drink, silly boy. We'll be at Bibi's in ten minutes. She'll have a kaapi and some naan ready for you when we get there."

"We're going to Bibi's?!"

"Unless you prefer to face your mom at your house, or my dad at mine . . ."

He nods. "Point taken."

The remainder of the drive passes in silence—with Walter occasionally taking large gulps of what he dubs "anti-inebriation awful-juice"—and then they're parked in Bibi's driveway and getting out of the car.

"Well, this is the cutest house ever," Walter says, and

Shelbi smiles. Because he's right: Bibi's one-story house in Morningside is brick and brown and cozy, and Shelbi can't wait to step inside, where she knows it smells like incense and blended spices. It's one of her favorite places on earth, second only to her rendezvous point with the universe.

Once they enter and take their shoes off, Shelbi leads Walter to a seat in the kitchen dining nook. Bibi comes over with the steaming kaapi and plate of buttered naan and sets them on the table in front of the drunken boy, and then she takes his chin and tilts his head back to shine a little flashlight into his eyes. "Wow, Walter!" She stretches to her full five-foot-one and puts her hands on her hips (side note: Bibi is the only other person on earth Shelbi would let call him "Walter"). "You're really sloshed!"

Shelbi snorts, and Bibi grins and shakes her head. "But don't fret, young man. Your beloved and I will take excellent care of you—"

"Bibiiiii," Shelbi whines, embarrassed.

Which is when she notices Walter's quivering chin.

He stuffs a piece of the bread in his mouth and chews, chews, chews. Bibi can also tell he's about to crack: she kisses Walter's forehead, then looks into her granddaughter's eyes and smiles. "You have such a beautiful soul, Walter." She touches his cheek and walks away.

The moment she's out of the room, he crumbles. "Everything is shit, Shelbi. Crap, I just cussed at you. I'm so sorry."

"We should go to the family room."

The moment Walter's butt hits the couch cushion, he starts sobbing.

"Aww, Walter!" Shelbi reaches out and pulls him into her arms, which seems to make him cry harder.

"We didn't mean for it to happen, Shelbi. It was just one time. *One time*."

Shelbi rubs the top of Walter's arm. "You didn't mean for what to happen, Wal-Wal?"

"The whole thing with Stephanie." He sniffles . . . and then starts wailing again.

"Stephanie, your ex-girlfriend?"

"Yeah. I saw her today. Well . . . yesterday? What even time is it? Oh God, my parents are gonna flip."

"I talked to your dad already. He knows where you are. What's this about Stephanie?"

Does Shelbi feel tacky for gently prodding? Slightly. But lately there's been this heat behind her breastbone at the thought of Walter's ex-girlfriend. And now she *needs* to know what's going on.

"Seeing her just reminded me of everything."

"What's 'everything,' love?"

Another sniffle, and then he sighs and sits up. "Have you read *Swirl?*"

"*Swirl?*"

"Yeah. The last book in the White Gangsta series."

Shelbi thinks for a moment and then . . . oh. "Is that the one where the little girl gets sick?"

"Yeah. Connor and Tay-Tay's daughter."

"Ugh. I'm sorry," Shelbi says. "If I knew you were reading it, I would've warned you about that part."

"Yeah, but then Quantavious . . ." And he stops.

"Quantavious? Doesn't he end up in jail?"

"He does, but not before the thing with Mercedes."

"The side chick? What about her?"

"The thing with the baby. I . . . well, Stephanie . . ." Walter puts his face in his hands. "And then seeing how wrecked Mercedes was after the whole procedure . . . Man, I just really messed up."

Shelbi's heart rate picks up pace as she puts it all together. "Stephanie got pregnant?"

Walter looks at Shelbi then, and his eyes are so full of sadness, she knows without a doubt that *she'll* soon be crying.

"Do you hate me now?"

"What? No! Of course not, Wal-Wal!"

He shakes his head, and his focus shifts to the opposite end of the room. "It was a little less than a year ago. Our relationship was falling apart because of, like, distance and stuff. And we thought maybe if we—well, you know. But we were dumb and didn't use any, uhh . . . preventative measures."

"What happened after she found out?"

"We went to her dad together. I was prepared to step up, Shelbi. Yeah, we were only seventeen, but we like . . . formulated this whole plan," he says. "Her dad told her she had to terminate. Said if she refused, he would never speak to her again."

"Wait, for *real?*"

"Steph's mom died when she was fifteen, so it was a total punch to the gut for him to say that to her, you know?"

"Wow."

"I tried to talk her out of it. I told her we could handle things. I even went to my super 'pro-life' mom and tried to get her to talk to Mr. Locke. You know what she said?"

Shelbi braces herself for what she's sure is going to make her erupt with rage. "Tell me."

"She said, 'Stephanie is Jacob's daughter, not mine, Andrew. I have no say in this decision.'"

Shelbi can't even . . . What is *with* this woman? "Man, I never thought I would say this 'cause I'm all for Black women supporting Black women, but your mom is *super* not my favorite."

"Oh, it gets worse. Not even a month later, when she decided to run for Senate, she made the asshole her campaign manager. All this 'life begins at conception' stuff she spews on television, and she wouldn't even fight to save her own grandchild. And I just *capitulated* like Mommy's Little Golden Boy. Even went along with her decision not to tell my dad."

"Five points for the SAT word. Does Charlie still not know?"

"Doesn't have a clue. Steph and I broke up, and I just moved on with my life like nothing happened. Stuffed it down so well, I didn't feel any grief over it until Emma died."

There aren't really any words to say, so Shelbi rubs circles on Walter's back.

"When I saw the way Quantavious manipulated Mercedes into ending her pregnancy to cover his cheating tracks, something cracked inside me. And then the next thing I knew, Steph and her dad were sitting in my living room."

"So you called trusty ol' Marcus." Shelbi shakes her head as a knot of guilt forms in her own stomach. Maybe he would've called *her* had she not been dodging him.

Ugh, too many *feelings*.

"And now here I am: rolling up into your adorable grandmother's lovely home *sloshed*, as she put it," he goes on. "Shelbi, I didn't even try to save my kid! Steph needed me to stick up for her, and I didn't. And then I *fell asleep* and let my little sister die. And then! Here *you* come being this brilliant burst of light in my life that I certainly don't deserve, and I clearly messed *that* up somehow because you just stopped talking to me for four whole days—"

And Shelbi can't hold it in: she bursts out laughing.

"It's not funny, Shelbi!"

She gets down on the floor in front of Walter so she can look into his face. "First of all," she begins, taking his hands in hers, "if you're under the impression that my 'adorable grandmother' has never seen or taken care of a *sloshed* teenager before, you are wildly incorrect. Bibi came to stay with us in California for a bit, and was typically the person holding my hair while I puked up Everclear."

"Ever *what*?"

"You don't wanna know. Second, we've been over this Emma thing before, Wal-Wal: if you're going to blame yourself, you have to blame everybody. Yes, you fell asleep. And yes, she died. But the best thing you can do about that now is accept it, forgive yourself, and try to get some peace about it."

"But, Shel—"

She holds up a finger and continues. "Now, with the Stephanie thing . . . Wal-Wal, the moment *she* made the decision to go through with the abortion, there's really nothing *you* could've done about it."

"But—"

"You said you tried to talk her out of it and were unable to, yeah? Her dad was making her choose between him and the baby—"

"A baby that was just as much mine as it was hers—"

"I know, Wal. *And* the baby was inside *Steph's* body; when it comes down to it, she had the final say. Not you. Not even her dad. *She* did."

He starts weeping again. So Shelbi returns to the couch, stretches out, pulls him into her arms so he's lying on her chest, and rubs circles on his back. "And as for that last thing, I needed to like . . . pull myself together is all," she says. "I'm sorry for ghosting you."

"You really suck for that, you know."

And now Shelbi's tears come.

"I forgive you, though," Walter says.

For a few minutes, they just lie there, breathing together.

Which is far more wonderful than Shelbi would like for it to be. Then it hits her: "You should give him a name. Or her. Or them."

"What?"

"The baby. You should give the baby a name. Express your love and apologize. Write a letter or something. Maybe it'll help with the guilt and grief."

"Connor," Walter says.

"Huh?"

"I've decided he's a boy and I'm naming him Connor. Though he's clearly not going to be a white gangsta."

Now Shelbi is cracking up. "And *there's* my best friend, Walter. Ridiculous as ever. Welcome back."

"Hey, Shelbi?" His words are getting heavier, and she knows he'll be asleep soon. Which means she should probably get up, so he doesn't fall asleep literally *on* her.

Can't say she wants to, though.

"Hmm?"

"You're really soft. And warm. And your heartbeat sounds nice."

"Uhhh . . . thanks, I guess?"

"I'm pretty sure I love you and you know it and that's why you stopped talking to me." He's slurring now, but Shelbi doesn't miss a single word. "But I don't even care because you're here now."

If Walter were sober, Shelbi might tell him the truth: she *did* in fact pull away as a result of . . . strong feelings. That felt big and unwieldy.

But it was *her* feelings that scared her. Not his.

Now, though, Shelbi lets his words sink in and realizes she can't panic because she's too comfortable. It feels good—*safe*—being wrapped up with him like this.

"Will you tell me a story?" he mumbles.

Shelbi laughs. "What kind of story?"

"A love one."

Her gaze is pulled across the room, and she smiles. "Did you happen to notice the picture over the mantel?"

"Nope. Everything's a little fuzzy."

She chuckles. "Okay, well, in the picture, Bibi is standing cheek to cheek with a man who's as big as my dad, but with darker skin and hair sprinkled with gray. That's my granddaddy. Bibi followed her older brother here from India to go to college, and she studied at Georgia Tech for two years, but then she sat down in the front row of Granddaddy's Intro to Nuclear Physics class—he was the professor."

Shelbi can feel Walter smile. "For real?" he says.

"Yep. Halfway into the first semester of her third year, she dropped out, and they got married. If you ask her about it, she'll say, 'Oh, there was no re*sist*ing. My Charles had skin the color of a coffee bean and teeth like the freshest milk.'"

Now Shelbi's getting all emotional again. "They were so in love, Walter. Like for-real soul mates. He was almost eighty when he died four years ago, but he would still chase her around the house dragging his oxygen tank behind him, and she would giggle as she pretended to run away. They'd been married fifty years by then."

"Hey, Shelbi?"

"Yes, Wal?"

"That was a great story."

"Thank you," she says.

"Shelbi, one more thing . . ." (This guy is *so* close to gone.)

"Yes?"

"Can you please not friend break up with me?"

"Huh?"

"You know," he says. "'Cause I broke rule number six?"

Before Shelbi can open her mouth to respond, Walter is gently snoring.

PHASE 3

Nuclear Fusion

ANDY—

who is standing at his bathroom mirror, brushing his hair—
now knows beyond a shadow of a doubt that he was not, in
fact, in love with Stephanie Locke. He can't put words to
what he felt for her, but in comparison to what he feels for
Shelbi Camille Augustine, Andy might as well have been
asleep through the entirety of his previous relationship.

In fact, if Andy *could* be with Shelbi every moment of
every day forever, he would. (Not that he'd ever *say* that
to anyone—it sounds stalkerish and maniacal even inside
his head.) He would take her beautiful places and buy her
beautiful things, all the while letting her know that *she* is
more beautiful than any and all of the beautiful things on
earth combined.

But he can't do any of those things.

For one, he's pretty sure she wouldn't like it. Despite her
confession that she has "also developed very strong feelings" for him over text the morning after she rescued him
from Marcus's house, she is insistent that they "remain
more or less in the Friend Zone, just with softened physical boundaries."

For two, even if she was like "Yes, Walty Wal-Wal" (he
loves when she calls him that) "I would love to be your
girlfriend," Andy doesn't have the kind of money it would
take to do all the things he'd like.

And then there's the for three: he's grounded until he goes to college. Literally.

Falling asleep *on* Shelbi Augustine—who smells like the honeysuckle flowers he used to pluck from the bush in his grumpy grandpa Walter's backyard—was by far *the* most pleasurable experience of his entire life. But waking *up* to Mr. Charles Andrew Criddle standing over him, plaid-covered arms crossed and a look on his face that could ignite a polar ice cap? Yeah, not so great.

Andy's pretty sure the only reason his dear ol' dad didn't throttle him (to death) the moment he opened his eyes is that Bibi happened to walk up, kaapi in hand, and say, "Ah, the memory of being young and how it keeps us humble. Wouldn't you agree, Charlie?"

Bibi, in fact, might've done even more than save Andy's literal life: he's got a feeling that youthful-memory recall she triggered for Dad is the sole reason he's allowing Andy to—

The doorbell rings, and Andy freezes.

For a beat too long. "Andy? You in here, son? Your guest is here . . ." comes Dad's voice through the (thankfully) closed bathroom door.

He's gotta get out there before they waltz into his room and she starts looking around. Needs to be ready in case of questions, comments, or concerns.

She's stepping in as Andy steps out. When their eyes meet, Shelbi smiles. And Andy instantly thinks he might be dead.

Dad says, "You two enjoy your movie," and gives Andy one of those *I'm trusting you to keep Jesus at the center* looks. Then he's gone (door stays open, of course).

And there she is.

Shelbi's hair is in a messy knot on top of her head, and she's wearing leggings (Leggings! Andy swears she's trying to kill him) with one of those hybrid top things that's too long to be a shirt but too short to be a dress. "First-floor bedroom with a window," she says, shaking her head. "It's a good thing you're the golden boy, Walter . . . your folks are just *asking* for trouble with this setup."

Speaking of trouble, Andy is trying *not* to feast his eyes on her splendor, but that comment from her triggers a highlight reel of scenarios involving the king-size bed Andy sees in his peripheral vision and will now struggle to ignore. Shelbi continues to look around, and then . . . "Geez, Wal-Wal . . . you think your bed is big enough?"

Fantastic.

Andy doesn't* respond, and now Shelbi's walking around his domain with her hands behind her back looking at his stuff: DVD rack, bookcase, judo trophies . . . It takes everything he's got to keep his eyes above her neck.

And then she completes her circle of the space and comes to stand in front of him. *Really* close. Like he's sure she can see straight up his nose.

---

* can't be trusted to

"Nice room." And she smiles.

"Uhh . . . thanks, I guess . . ."

Then Shelbi slips her arms around Andy's waist, presses her entire body against him, and *hums* as she exhales and lays her head against his chest. He's so startled (you know, considering the time he just spent trying to wrestle a leash onto his imagination?), he freezes.

"Sorry for this," she says. "Invading your personal space, I mean. I missed you, Wal-Wal." She squeezes tighter.

"I missed you, too, Shelbi." As is quickly becoming evident in another region of Andy's body. "So you ready for the movie?" he says, reluctantly creating some physical space between them.

"I was thinking we'd do something else," Shelbi says. And she winks.

Now Andy's thinking the whole *Hey, come over and watch a movie with me in my room* thing may not have been the best idea.

"Something else?" *Man, is it hot in here?!*

"Mmhmm." Then she drops down onto the sofa, and the tension disperses. (Andy can't tell if he's more relieved or disappointed.) "This is my first time in Walter-world. What do you usually do to keep yourself entertained here in your personal prison?"

Besides read Shonda Crenshaw novels? Andy's eyes go to his PS1—the *original* PlayStation, thank you very much— and quickly cut away. "Not telling," he says. "You'll make fun."

She laughs. "Well, now you have to tell me." She pats the space beside her, so he goes over and sits. "So?" she says.

Andy feels like even the old console itself—which had been his dad's in high school—is about to laugh at him. "*Mortal Kombat*," he replies.

"What's that?"

His head whips right. "You don't know what *Mortal Kombat* is?!"

"Nope."

And now Andy's laughing. "It's arguably the foremost classic fighting game to ever grace a gaming console."

She nods. "Well, let's go then." She stretches her wrists out and starts rolling her neck. As though preparing for *literal* combat. "Where's the controller thingy? I hope you're ready to get your behind whooped, Walty . . ."

Now Andy is *really* laughing. "Shels, you didn't even know what it was until fifteen seconds ago, and now you're trash-talking?"

"Go ahead and underestimate me, Criddle."

Still laughing, Andy turns on the TV and passes Shelbi a controller. After pushing her glasses up on her nose, she furrows her brow and examines it from all angles. "So, there are twelve buttons and two joystick dealies on this thing? Piece of cake. Don't forget, Walty, I live for a good algorithm. You'll win the first couple rounds, but it won't take me long to figure out the button combos and permutations."

Laughing, laughing, laughing. "All right then, nerd. You're on."

The game loads, and then they get to the character-choosing screen, and she balks. "Clearly these game designers never heard of a *sports bra*." She shakes her head. "Misogyny at its finest. Now I'm really gonna kick your butt."

And . . . she does.

Four rounds. That's all it takes. After four rounds, Shelbi Camille Augustine is kicking Andy's butt. Up, down, left, right, inside out and upside down. Shelbi's *so* good she even figures out three—THREE!—fatality-inducing moves Andy didn't know existed. Her impractically dressed female character lands another roundhouse kick to Andy's character's head and hits his ego simultaneously.

Sabotage is the only option.

When the big rumbly voice says *"FINISH HIM"* for the twelfth time in a row (*Seriously?!*), Andy drops his controller, jumps on her, and starts tickling.

"You CHEATER!" she yells. And so he tickles her some more. She's laughing the laugh that adds twinkle to the stars, and the fact that Andy's drawing it out of her with his fingertips makes him feel almost drunk with power.

They eventually end up on the floor in a full-blown tickle fight, and Andy vividly remembers "the talk" he and Stephanie had with their youth pastor where it was stressed just how dangerous tickle fights are for young couples who are trying to "live pure." (Not that they *succeeded* in that particular mission, but still.)

She shrieks and says, "Stop! Stop! You win!" and, victory secured, Andy relents.

But now she's beneath him on the floor, and he's looking into her eyes, and she's looking into his. Then there's this whispery voice in Andy's head that says *"Finish her"* like it does in *Mortal Kombat*. And caught in the moment, he looks at her lips and slowly closes in—

"Stop," she says.

So he does.

But he's so close, their noses are almost touching, and he can't seem to move. And now, frozen mere centimeters from Shelbi Augustine's face, Andy Criddle would like nothing more than to crawl under his bed and not come out until it's time for him to leave for Rhode Island.

But then . . . she smiles. "You know, your irises remind me of Jupiter's Great Red Spot. Which is really more *brown* than red."

"Are you even serious right now?"

"It's true!"

"So you're telling me I was half a second from kissing you, and you stopped me to make a comment about my *irises*? You truly *are* a nerd!"

Then, to Andy's utter shock (and slight dismay because he is *not* ready), Shelbi Augustine grabs his face and kisses *him*.

His lips really only part because he's so surprised. But the moment they do, she pulls the lower one into her mouth and gently bites down on it. Which . . . yeah, he should *definitely* get up. Except when he tries, she won't let him. "Mm-mm," she hums against his mouth.

So he quits fighting it. Shelbi Augustine continues to kiss him, and he kisses her right back.

And for the first time in as long as he can remember, Andy Criddle feels like he's getting something right.

Shelbi

. . . still can't believe she actually *did* that! And then *said* what she said once she and Walter finally de-suctioned their faces from each other: *That was kind of spectacular. Let's please do it all the time.*

Has she lost it?!

While yes: making out with Walter was *the* most gratifying experience of her young life (that boy is a fabulous kisser), Shelbi is on exceedingly dangerous ground. And she knows it.

She's back home now, wide-awake and staring at the ceiling with her fingertips tingling. Couldn't sleep if she wanted to. And she genuinely *does* want to . . . the brain reboot would be lovely. And helpful. But there's too much swirling around up in there.

She and Walter did wind up watching the movie—kicked

it old-school with Tobey Maguire's *Spider-Man*—and for the majority of it, she was tucked under his delightfully strong arm with the scent of his cologne in her nostrils. (She didn't know when he'd started wearing cologne— definitely a recent development—but she's glad he did because scent memory is huge for her. And now she has a *really* good one.)

She hated leaving. Like . . . hated it.

Which means the scary stuff has already started.

She'd told Walter rule number six had to do with her not wanting to do the whole relationship thing and therefore sticking to friendly feelings so things don't get weird . . . but there's actually more to it than that. Shelbi's been in therapy for three years now so she knows how important the concept of "self-awareness" is . . . and one thing she's *very* aware of is her tendency to get a little *too* into things that *feel* good. Like to the point where she wants said feel-good thing/experience/substance all the time. And it starts really messing with her if she can't have it.

Which makes Shelbi think about some of the ways "love" is described in books and music and poetry and stuff—the being "crazy in" it and "taken over by" it and "not being able to resist" it, and the fact that it's frequently likened to "madness." Shelbi Camille Augustine has experienced *real* madness. And it is *not* cool or fun or exciting.

She didn't tell Walter any of this because . . . well, it's kind of complicated to explain. *She's* still trying to get her head around how the chemicals in her brain interact with each other and how all that affects the way she feels. Her *mood*. Which is a thing that's tricky to even define.

How do you tell somebody *Hey, I really told you not to fall in love with me because I'm nervous I'll get addicted to you and literally lose it?*

Ugh.

He really is an incredible kisser. Super gentle and slow. Even *thinking* about it makes her . . . feel things. When it was time for her to leave and she tried to walk out of his room, he'd grabbed her arm to pull her back, and then caught her face and kissed her again.

Yeah, no words.

She sits up and swings her legs over the edge of the bed. Looks at the clock: 1:43 a.m. She hasn't been awake at this hour in a loooooong time.

Once they broke apart (again—and it's a miracle Charlie didn't see them . . . door was *wide* open), Shelbi looked Walter in the eye. "Wal-Wal?" she said.

"Hmm?"

"Can we still be us?"

(It's the most vulnerable she's been with him so far.)

His eyes went all melty. "Of course we can, Shelbi."

"No titles? I can't do titles, Wal . . ."

He laughed. "No titles necessary. Just don't go off dating other people without warning me first."

"Pshhh . . . you think I would go through this with someone *else*?"

He laughed, but she'd meant that. Because as wonderful as this *feels* at times, it's also excruciating. There's so much it's impossible to know.

Quietly as she can, Shelbi creeps downstairs to get her emergency ice pack from the freezer. She's sure Mama will notice it's missing in the morning, but hopefully she'll have found the words to express what she's thinking and feeling by then.

Back in her room, she lifts her shirt, lies down, and places the frozen, plastic-covered gel beads against the center of her chest. Her muscles instantly relax.

As she closes her eyes, something she's been trying to ignore for weeks drifts up to the front of her frazzled mind: Walter's drinking. It's been hovering there since the moment their mouths connected. No idea when he'd last had a drink, but she could taste the alcohol on his breath.

She inhales deep and lets the cold sink into her bones.

Kissing Walter, being close to Walter, smelling Walter, touching Walter, dropping her guard and letting Walter touch her . . . it all felt like magic.

But what happens if there *is* no rabbit in the hat? If she falls . . . and there's no one there to catch her?

Hi.

Well hello, beautiful.

You know, I kinda hate that your corniness moves me so powerfully.

Lol whatever.

You love it, and we both know it.

How was your appointment with Dr. Douglass?

Interesting.

That's actually what I'm texting about.

I learned some of the brain science of "being in love" today.

Oh boy . . .

You're totally about to ruin it for me, aren't you? Is it all a big lie?

I mean "ruin" is probably a bit strong, lol.

It's actually pretty cool . . .

In a nutshell, she explained that there are a LOT of brain chemicals involved in romantic love . . . adrenaline, serotonin, oxytocin, cortisol, testosterone, dopamine, epinephrine, norepinephrine, phenylethylamine . . . some go up, some go down, some spike during specific interactions (like kissing) while others drop . . .

Whole thing made me think about how new stars are formed and how it involves this perfect balance of chemical reactions between different elements.

Sorry, that was a lot.

You are THE most gorgeous nerd I've ever met.

Cut it out.

It's true. ¯_(ツ)_/¯

Well, thank you. You're not so bad yourself.

You trying to make me blush?

Cuz it's working.

Lol.

You know, Wal-Wal, you might have a special gift for derailing important conversations.

Sorry.

Just miss you 😊

I miss you, too.

Quite a bit actually.

While I'm trying to like . . . manage, I guess would be the way to put it.

Okay.

puts the conversation back on the right rails

What's going on, pretty lady?

I guess . . . well not to like kill the magic or whatever, but I did want you to know that I'm . . . adjusting.

Adjusting to?

You, silly.

Us.

All these new feelings.

Ah. Okay.

You said you wanted me to always be my true self, no holds barred. So I'm trying to stay up front about where I'm at.

Even though I'm nervous you're going to get mad at me for "ruining it" as you put it.

Oh man.

I'm sorry I said that. I didn't really mean it like THAT . . .

It's okay.

We're both adjusting. And if I've learned nothing else in therapy, it's that my fears are no one else's responsibility.

Okay. But I still want to do right by you.

So if I can help or even NOT do certain things, please let me know.

You're very sweet and I appreciate you.

There's not really a whole lot to DO.

Just know that if I seem to be a little *off* or moving differently, it's because I'm literally adjusting to all these chemical shifts in my brain.

What does it feel like?

Well, I'm having to be super diligent about keeping a consistent sleep schedule.

Because there's a part of me that would prefer to just . . . not sleep at all.

Dang.

Yeah.

And full disclosure: talking to you and being around you feels REALLY good. Like dopamine goes bananas.

Okay . . .

Which means I'm currently having to resist a number of . . . urges.

No, I'm not going to tell you what they are. Get your mind outta the gutter.

I didn't even say anything!

You're a straight, cis 18yo boy, Walter.

Gimme a break.

Hahahahaha! Touché, Ms. Augustine.

Touché.

Soooo . . . you wanna come watch a movie later?

Oh my God. Did you read a word of what I just said?

Yup. All of them actually.

I'll be there at 7.

CURVEBALL.

It's been thirteen days of (mostly) bliss, and Andy Criddle has never felt more alive. And not *just* alive: being around Shelbi and learning more about her and seeing how much she's dealt with and overcome has made Andy *hopeful* for the first time since Emma's death.

In fact, it's late afternoon, and he's currently on his bike, headed downhill with the wind blowing in his face, en route to a place he'd never have expected to visit voluntarily.

The previous night, Andy, Shelbi, and the Dads went out to dinner. In addition to the very bizarre insta-bromance ("This whole thing is obviously kismet since we're both named Charles," Dr. Augustine said as he and Charlie sat checking their calendars to figure out when they could go ziplining together), feeling how *peaceful* things can be when everyone is on the same page lit a spark that caught Andy off guard: he really misses his mom and wants to smooth things over with her.

The sun is shining, the sky is a brilliant blue, and the birds are chirping (when's the last time Andy even noticed that?). Feels like a good omen. Dad left town this morning for a business trip, so Andy's decided to take the next few days to try to reconnect with his beloved mother. She was gone by the time he woke up (well, if she was even home last night), so Andy decided to bust out the trusty old mountain bike for the two-and-a-half-mile journey to the Cris Criddle campaign headquarters—aka what used to be his grumpy old namesake grandfather's house.

Andy sees Mr. Locke's car before he sees Mom's, and just like that, all his *mend the relationship* good-feels dissipate like wisps of steam. He shouldn't be surprised that Mr. Locke is here—this is the *campaign* office, and he is the *campaign* manager.

But the fact that he *is* here—that the woman who carried Andy in her womb hired the man who catalyzed the decision to have *Andy's* kid removed from his daughter's womb—reminds Andy of all the things about his mother that make him want to haul off and break a bunch of stuff. In this moment, he'd like to turn his bike around and scrap the whole *mother/son reconciliation* thing. Because it's obviously a terrible idea that would never work.

But then Andy thinks about something Shelbi said to him when he expressed how jealous he was of her relationship with *her* parents: as uncomfortable as it is, sometimes the best thing you can do for someone else—especially a parent—is to let them be right.

So. He takes a deep breath and heads up the walkway to the front door.

Andy's glad he thought to bring his keys because it's locked. Which is weird, but okay. "Mom?" he calls out once he's inside.

She doesn't answer, but Andy can hear her laughing down the hall.

Which is good. If she's laughing, she's in a decent-enough mood—hopefully.

Andy takes a few seconds to go over the little spiel in his mind one last time, and then heads toward the office. The door is cracked, and he gets a little burst of fortitude when he hears her laugh again from the other side of it.

"Hey, Mom, I—"

. . . must be in a *really* messed-up dream because when Andy pushes the door open, he sees his mother sitting on the desk with her topless back to the door.

And shirtless Mr. Locke is standing in front of her. Pants undone.

"ANDREW!" Mom shouts, and she tries to climb off the desk and grab her clothes from the floor simultaneously. Andy's too much in shock to try to catch her as she stumbles over a box of files and crashes headfirst into the bookcase.

Mr. Locke is so busy trying to cover his tracks, he doesn't even check to see if Mom is okay. "Now listen here, boy"—he misbuttons his shirt but tucks it into his pants anyway—"you keep your damn mouth shut, you hear me?"

"Don't talk to him like that, Jake!"

"Be quiet, Cris!" he hollers. "If you want to win this election, I'll talk to him any way I ple—*AHHHH!*" He screams because Andy has managed to get around the desk and *Tsuri Goshi* flip his country ass on top of it. It breaks under the impact.

Then Andy is storming down the hall to the front door. As his shaking hand wraps around the doorknob, he can hear her say something he wishes she'd said a long time ago: "Jake, you need to leave now!"

Too little, too late. For everything, Andy realizes. Especially when, as he's pulling the door shut, she sticks her head out of the office and yells, not *I'm sorry*, and not *Andrew, please forgive me*, but "Please don't tell your father!"

The ride home is a blur. In fact, Andy's not really conscious of anything until he pulls the box marked TROPHIES down from the shelf in his closet and finds it empty. Hole behind his dresser is empty too: he actually tossed the last bottle that was in there after Shelbi left his house post–*Mortal Kombat*. His entire liquor stash has been cleaned out. Which makes Andy wonder if somehow Dad knew something bad was going to happen while he was gone.

No matter, though.

Andy treks down to the basement, opens the storage closet there, shifts a few things around, and opens one of the boxes of stuff moved here from Grandpa Walter's house when Mom made the place her headquarters. Right where Andy hoped it would still be is a dusty—but full— bottle of brandy. He knew it was in there because he was the person charged with moving this set of boxes.

Andy opens it and takes a strong swig . . . and gags. It's probably a hundred years old, and it tastes the way the inside of his judo bag smells after sitting in the corner for a week. But it's more than enough to get him sufficiently smashed.

So smashed, in fact, he can barely turn his head when his bedroom window opens who knows how many hours later—though it looks like dusk outside—and a brown-skinned girl with cat-eye glasses and really nice legs climbs into his room wearing what appears to be his judo hoodie.

What the hell?

She smiles, and Andy sees dimples, and it clicks: *Shelbi.* But when their eyes meet (sort of), she stops short and hers get really big.

She rushes over and tries to take the almost-empty bottle out of Andy's hand, which is like a twelfth-degree party foul.

"Leave me alone." Andy hear the words hit the air before he fully thinks them, if that makes any sense. (And even if it doesn't, it's whatever.)

Anyway, the girl—Shelbi—draws back.

Andy has hurt her feelings and he can tell. There's a little voice somewhere in his brain fog telling him to watch what he says, but screw that. He wants to be alone right now, and this girl is screwing everything up.

"Wal, what's going on?" she says. "I've been calling you all day. Is your phone off or something?"

She's giving Andy a headache. He wants her to stop talking.

But of course she doesn't. "I know Charlie left today, so I got a little worri—"

"You need to leave, Shelbi."

Why does she look so wounded? It's pissing Andy off. She invades his space and then has the nerve to look sad when he tells her to leave? What is *with* this chick? What's with girls—women—in general? Why do they do such messed-up things?

And why does Andy feel guilty all of a sudden? He's so sick of feeling guilty for crap that isn't his fault . . .

"Wal?"

"I DON'T FUCKING WANT YOU HERE, SHELBI!" he shouts, standing up. But too fast: he stumbles forward and has to catch himself on the dresser where the TV sits. "Just *LEAVE*, okay! And don't come back!"

She swipes at her eyes and makes a break for the bedroom door, but Andy doesn't like that. What if his mom—if you could even *call* *Congresswoman Cris Criddle* that— just happens to pull in the driveway as soon as Shelbi steps out the front door? Can't have that.

"No. What is *wrong* with you? Go out the same way you came in!" he barks. "And make it quick. I don't want to look at you anymore." *Or any other person with lady parts, for that matter.*

As she climbs back out the window, Andy takes another swig for posterity's sake. *Connor, this one's for YOU, buddy. Your mom, grandma, and country deadbeat ass grandpa didn't give a damn about you—or me—but I sure did.*

Andy turns on the TV—there's an error message because the Wi-Fi needs to be reset.

What.Ev.Er.

He takes one final long pull from the bottle. Then he leans his head against the couch cushion, shuts his eyes, and lets the liquor pull him under.

Fruition.

Shelbi has taken five showers in just over two hours, but she still feels unclean.

She should've known. She should've known when he didn't answer any of her calls today that he was bailing.

She *did* know. She knew something like this would happen. She *knew* he couldn't handle this. Couldn't handle *her.* It's not like the signs weren't there. Dude can't even face his *own* problems. What the hell made her think he would be there when *she* was dealing with something?

He *seemed* invested. He really did. Caring. Careful, even. She *thought* he was paying close enough attention to know when—

This is Shelbi's own fault. Because she *knew.* He said he loved her. That he'd fallen *in* love with her. But Shelbi knew he wasn't supposed to love her like that. She's known all along that it wouldn't work. These things never do, do they?

How could she have been so stupid?

Shelbi *KNEW.* She knew and she let her guard down anyway.

And now it's all over.

This whole thing was a terrible mistake.

WAKE-UP.

Someone's knocking.

"Andy?"

Sounds like Dad. But Dad's out of town . . .

The door creaks and Andy's bed shifts as someone sits down on it. And starts shaking him. Ugh.

"Andy, are you all right?"

It is Dad. Weird.

Andy turns to face him. "What are you doing here?"

"Last I checked, I live here, son."

"But your trip . . ."

"Is over. What's going on with you, Andy? What happened between you and Shelbi?"

Shelbi. Andy misses her. He wishes she were here . . . wait, she *was* here. Andy remembers she was here. Last night? But she left. Why did she leave? He can't remember.

He needs to get out of bed. Sitting up now. Man, does he have a headache.

Dad draws away from Andy and covers his nose. "Whoa, when's the last time you had a shower, son?"

"Huh?"

He's looking at Andy really intently now . . . which is scary for some reason. What's happening? Why is Dad here?

"What time is it?"

Dad looks at his watch. "Eleven forty-two a.m.,"
he says.

"What are you doing here, Dad? I thought you had
a business trip—" Andy rubs his eyes. He's gotta pull it
together.

"I just told you my trip is over, Andrew. Now tell me
what happened with Shelbi."

"With Shelbi?"

"You two broke up, didn't you?"

Okay, *now* Andy is awake. "Huh?" *Not that we were actually together . . . but still.*

Dad's eyes narrow. "Andy, I got a phone call from Dr.
Augustine a couple days ago telling me Shelbi wouldn't
come out of her room because something had happened
between you two. Dr. Augustine said he tried to call you,
but your phone went straight to voice mail. I tried to call
you too . . ." Dad holds up Andy's cell phone. It's dead.

Dang. "I guess I forgot to charge it."

"I can see that." He plugs the phone in using the cord
on Andy's nightstand. "I called your mom and she said you
were fine, but from the smell of things that's not the case."
Now he shakes his head. "Has your mom even been home?"

Mom.

Campaign office.

Mr. Locke.

Now Andy remembers. And he thinks he might throw
up . . . well, if his stomach weren't so empty . . . when's
the last time he ate?

He looks away from Dad because—duh—now that Andy remembers, making eye contact with the old man is impossible. "You talked to Mom—" *who is cheating on you with the hick-spawn of Satan?*

"Andy . . ."

Uh-oh . . . Andy can see the vein in Dad's neck bulging like it does when he's fighting the urge to throttle his beloved only son.

Something's not right. What was he saying about Dr. Augustine?

"As I said, I spoke with your mother on Saturday—"

Saturday?!

"What day is it?"

Now Dad's looking at Andy like Andy's totally lost it. "It's Monday, son."

"Monday?" Which would mean . . . Andy's been in bed for two and a half days?! Did he even get up to pee? He lifts the cover to look down at . . . Yeah, definitely (somehow?) got up to pee. But when?

Dad stands up. "All right, kid, that's enough. You know I've typically got your back, but I'm not liking the way these pieces are adding up. You don't know what day it is, you clearly haven't showered in quite some time . . . You been drinking again, Andrew?"

Andy swallows. Hard. He's never really been one to lie to Dad, but what else is he supposed to do? Admitting to a binge right *now* probably isn't the move. Where is that liquor bottle? He hopes he threw it away . . .

204

He gulps. "I, uhh, had a rough day on Friday. And . . ." *Here goes.* "Well, I'll admit I *wanted* to drink, but I, umm . . . I couldn't find anything in the house. Guessing you cleaned it all out?"

At this, Charlie softens, and Andy instantly hates himself. Dad being the softie always worked because Mom never had a problem playing bad cop.

Still, though: despite the truth being on the tip of Andy's tongue, he swallows it back down. "Guess I've been thinking about things so much, I lost track of time."

Now Dad looks sympathetic. He sits back down, but away from Andy. Does he smell *that* bad? Maybe he *didn't* get up to pee.

"I understand, son. Can you at least tell me what happened?"

Oh God . . . What the heck does Andy say now? Mom asked him not to tell *her* dirty (filthy!) little secret, but should Andy tell Dad anyway? It'll break Dad's heart, and who knows what he'll do . . . He's never been the violent type, but it's impossible to know how people will respond in situations like these. Andy also has no clue what happened with Shelbi, so he can't say anything about that either.

He has to stall. "What happened with what?"

Seriously, Criddle? You couldn't do any better than that?

"With Shelbi, Andy. Tell me what happened with Shelbi. Why'd you break up?"

Andy shuts his eyes, trying to remember . . . *something.*

Anything, really. Hopefully it just makes him look like he's devastated and needs a moment to process.

Little pieces come back: Andy, drunker than he's been in a very long time. Shelbi coming through the window. Shelbi looking hurt . . . and Andy being kinda mad about that? Shelbi exiting out the window. No Wi-Fi so no TV to watch.

And now Dad's saying they "broke up"?

What the hell did Andy do?

"This is going to sound weird, Dad, but I don't know if I knew we were broken up." Can you "break up" if you're not technically "together"? Did Shelbi and Andy cross over into "together" without Andy realizing it? Man, this is so confusing.

"Look, Andy: I don't know what happened or what you said or did, but when I spoke to Dr. Augustine again yesterday—that's Sunday, in case you were wondering—he said Shelbi had been in her room since Friday evening. He was on the verge of breaking the door down. Hasn't updated me since."

Andy's phone cuts on . . . and starts dinging like mad.

He freezes.

"You should maybe check those," Dad says.

But . . . well, Andy's afraid to.

"I know that sounded like a suggestion, but take it as an order."

Andy gulps and reaches for the device.

Shelbi?

Listen, I know you probably don't want to talk to me but . . .

I just really need you to answer.

Please, Shelbi . . .

I need to know you're okay.

I honestly don't remember what even happened on Friday but it obviously wasn't good.

And I would like to tell you how sorry I am.

Preferably to your face . . .

Shelbi, pleeeease.

Will you please, please respond?

I know I messed up. I know.
I promise I know.

But I need to know you're okay.

Shelbi.

Please.

Darkness.

CLARITY.

En route to the Augustines' that afternoon, Andy reads back through the messages he missed while blacked out . . . for two and a half *entire* days.

FRIDAY

BECKY

Hey, did something happen between you and Shelbi? She's acting strange . . .

7:16 p.m.

BECKY

Helloooo? Are you getting my messages? I need to know if Shelbi was all right the last time you saw her, Andy.

9:06 p.m.

MARCUS

Soooo some girl just called me looking for you? Said something about being Shelbi's cousin? You out here rollin like THAT, my guy??

10:30 p.m.

SATURDAY

MARCUS

Midas, u aight, bro? Homegirl called again . . .

12:32 p.m.

BECKY

Where u at, Grandpa?

1:17 p.m.

DAD

Andy, is everything okay? Spoke with Dr. Augustine, and he says something happened with you and Shelbi?

5:23 p.m.

BECKY

Ur cruisin' for a bruisin', Grandpa.
Really need you to respond. Like . . .
yesterday.

8:04 p.m.

MARCUS

Midas, where ARE u, dawg?

9:21 p.m.

BECKY

Umm, so my cousin doesn't want to
talk to ME now. Need to speak with
you ASAP, homeboy.

9:22 p.m.

SUNDAY

BECKY

WHAT DID U DO 2 HER?

2:43 p.m.

DAD

> Andy, I need you to call me.
> Your mom says you're fine, but . . .
> I need to hear from you, son.

3:15 p.m.

MARCUS

> Midas, I came by and no one was
> home . . . though there was a short angry
> girl who claimed to be Shelbi's cousin
> (same one whose been calling me, I
> presume) banging on your door. Cute as
> hell, too. Where are u?

5:03 p.m.

BECKY

> U R DONE, Grandpa. D.O.N.E.

8:42 p.m.

Andy can feel sweat from his armpits rolling down his sides as they approach the Augustines' fancy gate in Dad's truck.

It's standing wide open. Sign number one that something is terribly wrong.

They pull up in front of the house and Andy opens his car door and has one foot hanging out when Dad's hand lands on his arm. "Be honest with her, okay, son?" he says. "It's the least you can do and the minimum she deserves."

It's like a sensei punch right in the sternum. Especially considering that Andy wasn't honest with *him*. "Okay, Dad. I understand."

Andy walks up between the massive columns and rings the bell.

The second sign things are no good: Shelbi's mom practically falls over from shock when she opens the door and sees him standing there. "Andy?"

"Hey, Mrs. Augustine . . . I mean Shonda. Is Shelbi home?"

The third sign: when Andy asks this, Shonda looks like he just slapped her . . . and then her head cocks to one side as her eyebrows draw together. "You mind coming inside for a minute?"

Oh boy. "Uhh . . . sure . . ."

Shonda waves at Dad before shutting the door behind Andy, and he follows her down the hall to the kitchen, where she pulls out a chair. So he sits.

She sits too. "Andy, did something happen between you two?"

"To be honest, Shonda, I don't know. I, uhh . . . I got some bad news on Friday, and I remember Shelbi coming by, but I have no idea what I said to her. Is she okay?"

Shonda's eyes narrow. "Is there a *reason* you don't know what you said to my daughter?"

Might as well tell the truth. "I'd been drinking."

Shonda nods. "I see. Well, we had to check Shelbi into the hospital last night, sweetheart."

As Shonda's words sink in, Andy looks out the glass doors to the pool and gets a chill. Emma. Shelbi. Where was he when they needed him?

Asleep.

"Is she—" Here come the tears. "Is she all right?"

Shonda takes a deep breath and stares Andy right in the eyes. Almost like she's trying to decide how much it's safe to share with him. Then she shakes her head and her chin drops. "She seemed a little off on Friday night, but we knew she had a lot going on, so we were trying to give her some breathing room. She didn't come downstairs at all on Saturday, but when yesterday afternoon rolled around and she was still in there, we knew something was wrong. Charles had to drill the lock off her bedroom door, and he found her curled up on the floor. We took her to the hospital because she"—Shonda sighs—"she had some open wounds. I don't even know where she got . . . whatever she used."

Now Andy's *really* crying. Silently, but the tears are flowing like freaking Niagara Falls. "This is all my fault. If I hadn't pushed her away—"

"Pushed her away?" Shonda's head lifts. "What do you mean?"

Man, this sucks. "Well, like I said, I'm not entirely sure what I said to her . . . but I do know I wasn't in a good space, and she left right after."

For what feels like three lifetimes, Shonda doesn't say a word. Just keeps staring into Andy's eyes. Andy wouldn't dare look away. "What *do* you remember, love?"

Andy takes a deep breath. "I know I got home from . . . where I'd gone and learned what I'd learned, and I was so overwhelmed by it, I just wanted to zone out. I'd had quite a bit to drink when Shelbi showed up, and I'm not exactly sure if she said anything to *me*. But the next thing I remember is her looking sad." He gulps. "And then she was leaving."

"Do you have a drinking problem, Andy?"

The question hits him smack in the middle of his chest. He remembers Shelbi asking him basically the same thing the first time she took him to her rendezvous point with the universe. He'd told her no, but . . .

Does Andy have a drinking problem? He can't bring himself to say no *now* because it'll sound like denial (and maybe is?), but he doesn't want to say yes, either, because that's kind of a big deal to admit . . .

"Umm . . . I'm not really sure?"

She nods. "Do you always get the urge to drink when faced with a problem you can't solve?"

Is Andy really having this conversation with Shelbi's *mom* (aka Shonda freaking Crenshaw)? "I guess. Well, at least since my sister died in March."

"Does alcoholism run in your family?"

"My grandpa Walter was an alcoholic when he was young, but he stayed sober for the last fifty years of his life." Then again, Andy did find that brandy in a box of his stuff . . . And not that the constituents could ever know, but Mom also has stretches where she'll drink an entire bottle of wine each night.

"You typically drink alone?" Shonda asks.

Andy nods. "Pretty much. Unless I'm at a party."

"And in secret, I presume?"

That one stings. "Yeah."

"And you said you don't remember what you said to Shelbi—"

"Or anything from the two days after that," Andy says, putting his head in his hands and letting the reality settle over him.

"Have you blacked out like that before?" Shonda asks. "Any other instances of short-term memory loss?"

Now he's crying again. "Mmhmm."

Shonda puts a hand on Andy's shoulder. "Has Shelbi ever told you that I'm a recovering alcoholic?"

His head pops up. *"Really?! YOU?"*

Shonda laughs, and with no other sounds around to distract him, Andy now knows where Shelbi gets her sing-songy snicker from. "I've been sober for twelve years. Hid it pretty well initially—Shelbi's father had no idea until a couple years into our marriage."

"Wow," Andy replies. "So . . . what made you stop? If I'm allowed to ask that?"

She smiles. "You are. I lost Shelbi in a shopping mall when she was four years old," she says.

"Dang."

"You got that right. To this day, I attend Al-Anon meetings."

"Al-Anon?"

She nods. "They're designed for the family members of alcoholics. I went to AA for years, but happened upon an Al-Anon meeting back in Los Angeles. Now I prefer those because they remind me of how my loved ones would be impacted were I to give in to the urge to grab a bottle when the road gets a little rough."

"Ah," Andy replies.

"I'd like for you to come with me to the next one."

"Huh?"

Shonda puts her hand over Andy's on the table. "Baby, my daughter is an incredible young lady, and it's imperative that the people she lets in are able to take her circumstances seriously. Now, I don't say that to shame her. There's nothing shameful about one's brain chemicals getting a bit out of whack, and from the sound of it, yours are a little off at the moment too. I just need you to understand that being a *positive* force in her life will require a certain level of personal stability. And I think you might need some help of your own."

Andy sighs. "Yeah."

"Shelbi's dad and I try not to meddle too much in her personal life because that wouldn't be fair to her, but I *will* say you're not likely to see or hear from her for a bit. In the meantime, I want you to think long and hard about whether you're really prepared to deal with all *this* in addition to the personal problems you've already got going on. Not trying to offend you, sweetie. Just keepin' it real."

Shonda is staring at Andy again, but he knows she's not expecting an answer. Not yet, at least.

"Pass me your phone," she says, and so he does. She taps at the screen for a few seconds, then slides it back. "There. You have my number now. Let me know what you decide about accompanying me to a meeting."

"Yes, ma'am."

She rises from the table. "I have to get back to work. Do you need Mario to drive you home?"

"No thank you, Shonda. I'm sure my dad is still waiting out front."

"All right. You know the way out. Appreciate you coming by." She kisses Andy on the forehead.

As Shonda exits the room, Andy stands and looks out at the pool water and remembers that *don't fear the unexpected* stunt he pulled: where he scooped Shelbi up and threw her in to prove that he would jump in after her.

He shakes his head. Foolish to make a promise like that without knowing whether or not he can actually swim.

Disoriented.

It's strange to wake up in a place that feels, smells, and sounds very different than the one where you remember lying down, but even stranger is knowing that the moment you open your eyes, you're going to burst into tears. Like full-on sob session impending. You can feel it as surely as you feel the ache in your side where you added a few rungs to your ladder.

So you keep them closed.

And still, there's that knot at the base of your throat and it's starting to expand—

"Shelli Belli, you awake, love?"

Your daddy's voice.

You open your eyes, but it's too bright, so you shut them again. Too late, though: a whimper breaks through, and your eyes fill and overflow despite being closed. "Where am I?" You try to shift your body, but the burst of pain that shoots down your right side is so jarring and intense, you can't even cry out.

Your heart rate climbs.

"Whooooa, now, baby girl." Daddy's massive hand engulfs yours, and he gently squeezes. It works: you inhale deep. (Which might be a mistake. The lemon-doused bleachy scent in the air turns your stomach.) "It's all right. Everything'll be fine."

"Daddy?"

You crack. And now you're bawling.

"Oh no, honey . . ." Daddy tries to hug you, but it tweaks your side again. *Definitely* cry out this time.

"Oh, baby. I'm so sorry! Can you tell me what's the matter? Did something happen?"

You shake your head. "No. Just . . . wires all crossed." You sniffle. "In my brain." More tears. "No real *reason* to be crying, I just can't not."

Daddy nods. "Okay. I understand."

"How is Walter?"

There's no response. When you look at Daddy, he's staring off at something you can't see, with his thick black eyebrows pulled down and his jaw set tight.

"Daddy? Did you hear what I asked—"

"I heard you," he replies. "He's fine, last I heard. Your mama has taken him with her to a couple of her meetings."

You nod, and as you do, you can feel your mood shift. Where before there was just this nebulous urge to cry, now there's anger and sadness and hurt and shame. It was a mistake, getting close to him. "Can we go home now?"

Daddy shakes his head. "You're going to be transferred to the pediatric psychiatry ward tomorrow morning. Dr. Douglass asked them to keep you for a few days as you adjust to your new medication regimen. I found you—"

"I don't even wanna know," you say, putting a hand up.

And now you're tired again.

What a disaster.

"I have stitches?" you ask.

Daddy's chin drops. "Two sets."

You nod and close your eyes. And though you know it'll take weeks to detangle your emotions and get back on track, one thing rings crystal clear:

"Okay. I've learned my lesson."

PHASE 4

Supernova

ANSWERS (SORT OF).

Patterns. A word that came up in the Al-Anon meeting Andy attended with Shonda last night . . . and that's been poking at him like the Apostle Paul's thorn in the flesh. (Andy also went to church this past Sunday.)

A kid named Jeremy—who comes with his mom and little sister to discuss their dad's drinking—brought up *patterns* and really got Andy's wheels spinning.

To the point where he recognized one: the majority of the times that Andy has drunk himself stupid have been catalyzed by something involving Mom.

The most interesting thing is that when he mentioned all this to Shonda, she told him a story: "I started seeing a therapist after my sister died, and like you, I had a lot of anger toward my mother. And the therapist told me something I'll never forget: 'People aren't put on this earth to meet your expectations.'" It not only gave me the perspective I needed to let her *off* the hook, but to this day, it keeps me from putting anyone else *on* the hook. Myself included."

(Side note: Yes, Andy *does* sometimes feel a little weird about the fact that he confides in the mom of a girl he negatively impacted with his drinking . . . a mom who also happens to be his favorite author. Truth really is stranger than fiction.)

This morning, Andy took Shonda up on her offer to take him to an actual AA meeting . . . and for the first time ever, he admitted aloud that he *is* an alcoholic. And the moment he did, he knew it was time to have a chat with the congresswoman.

Now here he is: approaching the Criddle residence in the big Benz with Shonda beside him, trying to figure out exactly what he's going to say when the time comes.

When Andy sees Mom's car in the driveway, his heart climbs up into his throat; the fact that she's even home right now has to be some kind of sign. He just hopes Dad's not there.

"Mom?" Andy says as he walks in. "Dad? Are you here?"

No response. This is eerily similar to the scenario at the campaign office, and now Andy's palms are damp.

When he reaches the kitchen, the world turns upside down . . . well, at least it seems to: the kitchen table is overturned with one sad chair pinned beneath it, the crystal vase that usually sits at its center is in shards on the floor, and there are sheets of paper strewn everywhere. There's one of those sleazy tabloid magazines on the kitchen counter, and the headline reads like a scream: CONGRESSWOMAN CRIS CRIDDLE'S DIRTY LITTLE CAMPAIGN SECRET.

Oh boy.

"Mom, are you here?" Andy runs upstairs to his parents' room. She's not in there, but there are clothes and shoes all over the place.

God, this is not happening.

Not in the closet.

Not in the bathroom.

Back downstairs to check the home office she never uses anymore; not in there.

Basement? Nope.

Garage? Negative.

Andy's room? No.

Dang it.

Wait . . .

Andy races back up the stairs and throws open Emma's bedroom door. Mom is sitting criss-cross applesauce on Emma's My Little Pony bed hugging her Cabbage Patch doll, Baby. She looks at Andy for half a second and then fixes her gaze back across the room. "It's over," she says. "It's all over."

Andy takes the deepest breath imaginable and goes over to sit beside her. Rage is the first thing he feels—thirteen months of pent-up emotions will do that to a person—but rage would probably be counterproductive right now, so he leans into the second option: "Mom, are you all right?"

She shakes her head no.

"What happened?"

"I served your dad divorce papers."

"Divorce papers?"

She nods then. "I filed them last week. More for you and him than anythi—"

"How the hell does *you* filing for divorce benefit *us*?"

There's that rage again . . .

"I'm not good for this family right now, sweetheart," she says. "I haven't been for some time now."

"So you decided the best solution is *bailing*?"

She sighs.

"How long, Mom?"

"Hmm?"

"How long have you been having an affair with Mr. Locke?"

She doesn't answer immediately and Andy wants to scream at her, but he doesn't. He waits. Fifteen seconds . . . thirty . . .

"Since Emma died," she finally says.

"Why? Was Dad not enough for you?"

Now she's crying (though truth be told, Andy's not buying it). "Your dad is wonderful, Andrew. He's too good for me. I've never deserved him—"

"Mom, if you're going to spend this whole conversation feeling sorry for yourself, we can end it now."

She turns to look at him, and her eyebrows pull together. "You're different, Andrew."

"Yeah, I am. And I want to talk about this like adults. Why did you start sleeping with Mr. Locke? I mean of *all* people, Mom . . ."

"I can't really answer that, Andrew," she says, and she looks away again. "When your sister died, I just—I don't know. Since you want to talk like adults, I'll tell you: I miscarried a few times between you and Emma, and it was a *very* difficult pregnancy. After fighting so hard to have her here and then losing her anyway, I was just so *angry*."

Andy's stomach churns.

"It all happened so fast—when we left the bungalow, she was alive and happy and bouncing around as usual, but when we came back, she was—" She shakes her head. "I felt like I'd been hit by a bus, Andrew. I don't even know how to describe it."

She squeezes the doll to her chest, and Andy's guilt and grief over Emma's death rear their hideous heads. "I . . . I'm sorr—"

"Don't apologize," she says. "Anyway, your dad could see that I was falling apart, so he encouraged me to pull back from campaigning for a few months. The election isn't until November, so I could have. No one would've batted an eye. But Jake—"

"Please don't call him that."

"Fine—*Mr. Locke* said no. He told me to use it to my advantage . . . "*Grieving mother pushes through for the betterment of our nation.*"

Andy shakes his head, and wrath clacks around within it like a handful of marbles. "That guy is such a fucking asshole, I swear to God . . ."

"*Excuse you*, adults or not, I am still your mama and I will not tolerate that kind of language!"

"Sorry. I just really hate that guy. I can't believe you're cheating with *him*. I mean seriously, Mom, you couldn't pick *anyone* else?"

"As I was *saying*, Mr. Locke pushed me to keep going," she continues. "Hearing him tell me I didn't need a 'break,' that I was a strong, accomplished Black woman and I could show that strength by sticking things out—well, it did something for me. So I did. I 'pressed on,' as the Bible puts it. And the numbers began to tilt in my favor. Then one thing led to another."

"And what about Dad?"

She shakes her head again. "Things were already strained between your father and me, Andrew. Honestly, he didn't really want me to run for Senate, and I resented him for that. He asked me to pull back when your grandpa Walter died, but of course I didn't because I was so pissed the old bastard croaked before I could win this election—he was terribly hard on me, your grandfather. Nothing I ever did was good enough for him."

"*That* certainly doesn't sound familiar . . ."

"Huh?"

"Like father to his daughter, like daughter to her son. Please continue."

She's silent for a beat—hopefully picking up what Andy is laying down. Then she says: "When your dad suggested I take a break after Emma's death, I was okay with it at first, but then when Mr. Locke said the opposite, I felt like your dad was trying to manipulate me into dropping out of the race—"

"That's bullshit, and you know it, Mom. Dad loves you! He's been nothing but supportive—"

"You're right, and I can see that now. But the fact of the matter is Mr. Locke touched on a very broken place inside me at a very bad time. Is that an excuse for what I've been doing? No. But that's what happened."

Andy clenches his jaw to keep stuff he wouldn't be able to take back from exploding out of him.

"After you caught us, and I saw how hurt you were, I decided it was time to get myself together. I intended to formally drop out of the race and resign my congressional seat after speaking with your father, and I came in with the divorce papers this morning. But he had that darn tabloid in his hand when I stepped into the kitchen. The conversation didn't go very well, as I'm sure you could tell from the flipped table."

Andy snorts.

"I filed for divorce because I really do feel it's best, Andrew," she says. "You and your father deserve better than I'm able to give, and I can't handle the pressure of your expectations anymore. I cannot and will not ever be the wife your dad needs, honey. You will probably never understand that, and I'm not asking you to, but I need you to let me off the hook."

"So you're done with Mr. Locke, then?"

She hesitates, then her eyes drop to the floor, and the answer is clear. "It's complicated, sweetheart."

And now they're churning . . . the fury and the hurt and the resentment. Andy had no intention of talking about the thing that, to this day, twists his stomach into a thousand little knots of guilt and grief and regret. But he can feel it pushing up from his gut and squeezing his lungs and filling his throat. It's about to explode out of him.

Mom can see something's wrong. "Andrew, are you—"

"*Why*, Mom?" He stands up. "Why would you hire *him*, let alone cheat on Dad with him? HIM! The guy who runs around talking about how 'pro-life' he is, but manipulated his daughter into aborting our baby!" Andy's tears are flowing fast. "Why didn't you do anything to stop it? How can you lead a crusade to 'protect the unborn,' but not fight to save your own grandchild? How could you do that, Mom?"

"I don't know, Andrew."

"*What?*"

Now she's crying too. "I said I don't know! I don't have an answer for you."

"God, what *do* you know?"

She draws back, eyes wide, and Shonda's words ring through Andy's head like an alarm clock: *People aren't put on this earth to meet your expectations.*

Congresswoman Cristine Criddle certainly hasn't met Andy's "mom" expectations. Honestly, since he started high school, she hasn't really been around much. And *despite* Shonda's words, he really wants to say as much. In fact, he'd love to lay into her about a number of ways his expectations have gone unmet: she rarely ever came to his judo matches. She wasn't around when he needed help with homework. He has no idea how to deal with his emotions because she never really showed any besides irritation. When he *did* do well, she never said she was proud—only pushed him to "keep improving". . .

But then an image he isn't expecting pops to the front of his mind: the shift in her face from hope to despair when it was clear that Dad's CPR attempts on Emma were futile. She'd looked at Andy then, and he'd watched the light go out of her eyes.

It hits him then: he probably hasn't met her "son" expectations either. He surely also failed to meet Emma's "big brother" expectations, and he *definitely* failed to meet Shelbi's "friend" ones.

Man.

"I'm sorry for saying that," Andy says. He sits back down. "I guess it's okay that you don't know. I . . ." *Deeeep breath.* "Well, I guess I don't know why I do stuff either sometimes."

She doesn't reply, but Andy can feel some of the tension lift from the room. "You have my word that I'll do my best to let you off the hook," he says. "But you have to let me off too, Mom. That whole 'he's no son of mine' thing really sucks."

She nods. "You're right, and I'm sorry for saying that. You're an incredible young man, and I really am proud of you. I hope you'll forgive me for not saying it sooner."

Andy smiles. It's funny: now that she's giving him her approval, he finds that he doesn't actually need it anymore. "You know I love you, right, Mom?"

Another nod. "I love you, too, Andrew. I apologize in advance for the media storm that's coming. Hopefully you'll be able to escape it when you go to Rhode Island."

Now Andy laughs. In spite of everything else going on, Congresswoman Cris Criddle is thinking about the media. Guess you can take the congresswoman out of the Senate race, but you can't take the Senate race out of the congress-woman.

Andy kisses her on the cheek and gets up to leave the room. He's reaching for the doorknob when she says, "Andrew?" and he turns around.

"Yeah?"

She looks him right in the eye. "Honey, Emma's death wasn't your fault. I want you to know that."

And now Andy can't look away from her because that was unexpected and he wasn't ready for it. The strangest thing, though? He genuinely feels lighter.

"Thanks for that," he replies.

She nods, and it's clear there's nothing more to say.

So Andy walks out of Emma's room and pulls the door shut behind him.

Crossroads.

Shelbi sits at the Augustine kitchen table, picking at her oatmeal and staring out at the sun glinting off the pool. It's been two weeks since she was released from her (brief) stay in the hospital, and her side just spit out what she hopes is the last surgical stitch she ever sees in her life. She learned, upon having the bandages removed, that there were three new rungs on the ladder of scars that stretched from the top of her rib cage down over her hip . . . but what's missing is the memory of putting them there.

Which is probably for the best.

She sighs. Then holds up the little piece of knotted plastic thread, marveling that mere moments before, it was being used to hold her skin together.

"Eww, what even *is* that?" comes a voice from beside her.

"One of my stitches," Shelbi replies.

"Ummmm . . . *what?!* Oh my God," her (dearly beloved) cousin Becky continues, flapping her hands around like she's being attacked by flies or something. "I have to get away from you. Is your wound, like . . . gonna open up and start spewing blood everywhere?"

"You are so unnecessarily dramatic. It came *out* because my body doesn't need it anymore."

Becky shudders, and the girls lapse back into silence.

Shelbi chuckles. She really does appreciate her cousin.

The past couple weeks have given her a lot of time to think. And one of the conclusions she's come to is that where her interactions with other people are concerned, she doesn't want anyone treating her like she might break. No, living with "atypical" brain chemistry isn't always fun, but it also doesn't *have* to keep her from having an enjoyable life.

"So have you talked to Walter?"

"Andy," Shelbi replies without thinking. "I mean . . . Sorry." She shakes her head. "Whatever. No. I have not."

"Isn't he leaving for college soon?"

Shelbi shrugs despite the fact that her heart is beating a little faster at the thought. "How should I know?"

"Girl, bye. I don't know who you think you foolin' with all that *feigned* nonchalance, but you can definitely miss *me*. Tryna act like you don't care about that boy . . . Tuh!"

"He broke the contract, Becky."

Becky's eye roll is pretty next-level, even for her. "Contract, shmontract—"

"That's not a word."

"Don't do me, Shelbi. Let's not forget you had me read the thing before you even showed it to him. Do the same rules not apply to you? Because I'm pretty sure what *you're* doing would be considered ghosting, wouldn't it? Which rule was that? And we *all* know YOU broke the 'no falling in love' one. Which was a dumb—not to mention *presumptuous*—one to even have on there."

Shelbi grits her teeth. She hates talking about this. And

thinking about it. And acknowledging that it's even a *thing* at all. But it's not like Becky's saying anything untrue.

It's annoying.

Still, though. "Becky, Andy has his own demons to fight."

"Isn't he going to AA with your mom like twice a week?"

"Al-Anon. Which is different."

"Are you really diminishing this man's pursuit of sobriety?! I don't even know who you *are* right now!"

Shelbi sighs. And just like that, tears have sprung to her eyes. "Becky, I'm scared."

"Of?"

Shelbi shakes her head. "There's really no way, in this galaxy or the next, for me to explain what it's like to wake up in a hospital with gashes in your side that *you* put there," she says. "With zero recollection, Becky. When Andy reacted to me the way he did? My brain just flipped into doing its own thing. And took my body with it. It's absolutely terrifying."

Becky doesn't respond. (How could she?)

"There's a chunk of time that's just gone from my mind," Shelbi continues. "And then getting transferred to the psychiatric ward . . . It's not the easiest place to be, Beck. There are people—like *kids* our age and younger—who are dealing with *way* worse stuff than me through no fault of their own, you know?"

Becky's eyes drop. "Yeah."

"I've spent the past two weeks getting adjusted to med changes. I have no appetite. Sometimes I wake up in the middle of the night, drenched in sweat, and have to stick an ice

238

pack between my boobs to get my nervous system to calm down. It's a struggle to even get out of bed on some mornings, and on days when I get out just fine, it can be a struggle not to crawl back in and just . . . stay there. I really do need to stay away from *anything*—person, place, object, et cetera—that has the potential to trigger me the way he did."

It's quiet for a good bit, but then Becky sucks her teeth. And Shelbi instantly knows that her dear cousin is about to say something she won't like.

"Okay, hear me out," Becky begins. "Like, I hear you. I really do. You *do* need to avoid your 'known triggers,' as you put it. But also, like . . . cuz, I know you. And I *know* that what you're trying to present as some sort of mental health mechanism is partially you running and hiding."

"Beck, you don't—"

Becky puts a hand up to stop Shelbi. Then continues: "Yes: shit went left. And yes: Andy *does* have his own stuff to work through. But who doesn't, Shelbi? Haven't we all needed a second chance at some point or another?"

Shelbi's eyes narrow as she takes in what her cousin is saying. She's obviously not wrong: Most people *do* need a second chance. Or even a third. Shelbi included . . .

But this sort of *was* a second chance for her, wasn't it? She lowered her guard and let someone in even after what happened the last time.

And it happened again.

Were the circumstances different? Absolutely. But the outcome was pretty much the same: blackout, stitches in her side, hospitalization, medication changes, and an arduous (and ongoing) climb out of the pit of short-circuited brain chemicals. What person in their *right* mind would put themselves in a position for that to happen again?

Shelbi shakes her head. "Becks, the thing I know for sure is that what I was afraid would happen did. Walter is a great guy, but I definitely ignored some red flags that are staring me in the face now. Which is not a route I can take again."

"But, Shelbi, people *change.*"

"Yeah, I know. But *how* they'll change is impossible to predict," Shelbi continues. "Not that any of it even matters: He's about to go to Rhode Island, where I'm sure he'll meet plenty of great girls. We can both just . . . move on."

Becky stares at Shelbi. Clearly not buying any of what she's selling.

"How's Trish?" Shelbi says, needing the conversation to head in a different direction. She's been doing an excellent job of not thinking about the whole Walter situation, but it doesn't take much to get her crying these days. If she *really* gets going, which she knows would be the case right now, she'll wind up needing to lie down. The goal is to stay *out* of bed until this evening.

"Oh no, ma'am," Becky replies. "You not 'bout to live vicariously through *my* love life because you refuse to fix yours. Nope."

Shelbi laughs. "You're ridiculous."

"And you're a quitter."

It's a low blow, and Shelbi *knows* Becky knows it. But

she refuses to take the bait. "Hey, whatever it takes to stay alive," she says.

"Yeah, okay."

"You'll see." She swallows hard. (*No tears, Shelbi!*) "Walter and I cutting our losses is the best possible thing."

LOSSES.

Andy didn't expect to be this emotional. Like fine: watching your mom back a U-Haul filled with her stuff out of the driveway of the only house you've ever lived in isn't an everyday occurrence. But after everything *former* congresswoman Cris Criddle has put their family through, Andy thought he'd be more . . . numb.

Especially since he knows Dad asked her to wait to move out until after they'd taken Andy to college. Which is in just a few days. Her (clear) refusal—and the impression she gave that she might not be "well enough" to come on the trip—was just salt in the wound.

Well, in *one* of the wounds. At this point, Andy has more than he can count. It's actually a miracle he hasn't picked up a bottle and drunk himself into oblivion. It's safe to say this past year has dumped more loss and sorrow on Walter Andrew Criddle than he knew it was possible to experience. And every single bit of it has to do with people in possession of two X chromosomes.

First, he lost Stephanie (and Connor—who, for all he knows, was a chromosomally XX tiny human). Then Emma. And he really probably started losing Mom when *she* lost her dad, but now she's also *physically* gone.

In the thick of all this, Shelbi *found* him . . . and he, like an idiot, managed to lose her, too. Which is the one that hurts the most . . . though he's been trying to hold tight to Marcus's advice: *Man, don't sweat that girl.* For once it actually seemed sound, even though Andy's pretty sure Marcus's reason for giving it had more to do with ego protection than any sort of respect for Shelbi deciding to keep her distance.

It's hard, though. Real hard. He's been desperate to talk to her about all this mom stuff, and the lack of her calming presence makes him feel like he's crossing a battlefield covered in land mines, completely naked and with zero means of protecting himself. Dad's doing his best to be supportive, but he's obviously going through his own grief, so Andy tries to keep the additional load pretty light.

"Let's head on inside, son." At the sound of Dad's voice, Andy realizes the taillights of Mom's moving truck are long gone. He's just staring down an empty street. "We gotta start getting *you* packed."

"What if I don't wanna go?" The words surprise Andy as they hit the air.

Dad too, apparently. "Huh?"

Andy turns to look the old man in his blue eyes. "What if I don't wanna go to Brown, Dad?"

"Uhh . . . can we maybe talk about this *not* out on the front lawn?"

As they make their way inside, Andy's resolve strengthens. He's sure Dad will understand. He always does.

"Let's chat in the kitchen," Dad says.

"Okay."

Dad pulls Andy's chair out for him once they get there. "Now," he says, taking his own seat. "What's on your mind, son?"

Again in defiance of his own expectations, once Andy opens his mouth, a bunch of feelings he didn't realize were in him start pouring out. "What if I don't want to go, Dad?" he says. "I only applied to Brown because it was Mom's alma mater and she wanted me to. Besides, it's like a billion miles away, and I don't like the idea of *you* being here all by yourself? *And* it's gonna be really cold there in the winter . . . you know how I feel about snow—"

"Andy?"

"Yeah?"

Dad puts his hand over Andy's on the table. "You're upset, son. It's okay to just say so."

And that does it. Andy completely loses it.

No idea how he even gets there, but the next thing Andy knows, he's wrapped in his dad's arms on the couch, sobbing like a newborn baby. There's drool and snot and eye gunk galore. Dad's rubbing his back, but when Andy looks up and sees that the old man is crying too, it unleashes something wholly different.

"How could she just *leave* us?" Andy says. "How could she *walk out* like we're not her family?" He's talking about his mom, yes. But as it spills out of him, he realizes he's also pretty mad at Shelbi. Does that anger feel justified? Not necessarily. But there's no denying it's there. "Why do all the women I love leave me, Dad?"

Dad takes a deep breath and it hits Andy: the reason the whole flipped-table thing was so wild is because Andy's never really seen Charlie Criddle *mad* mad before. Guy's keeping his cool even now. "It's complicated, Andy," he says. "Most things involving other people usually are. Your mom's not well, son. She hasn't been in quite a while now. I've known and seen it, but she needed to see it for herself before she was willing to take any action."

"But aren't you mad?"

"Of course, I'm mad, Andy," Dad says. "I gave your mom everything I had for almost twenty-five years. This might be the maddest I've ever been in my entire life."

"So like . . . why aren't you flipping out or something?"

"Ah, what good would that do? Certainly won't change anything. World's still spinning, and I've got a kid to take to college." And he gives Andy a good squeeze.

"Dad, I'm not going."

"You sure are."

"But, Dad—"

"We leave in three days' time."

Now Andy sits up. "Dad, I don't want to go to that school."

"I understand that. You can transfer wherever you'd like

after the first semester. But you're definitely going. You've worked too hard and come too far not to, and Criddles don't renege on our commitments—*no shade* over your mom, or whatever the hell you kids say these days."

Andy can't help it: he snorts.

"All I ask is that you give it your best shot while you're there. Deal?"

Andy looks at his dad. A man dealing with way worse than a girl he likes rightfully not speaking to him after he got trashed and crushed her sweet soul. A man who, despite being the very best guy Andy knows, lost his daughter *and* his wife without doing *anything* wrong. A man who has his back and doesn't judge and loves him better than anyone ever has.

"You know I love you, right, Dad?" he says.

Dad nods. "Mmhmm. Now prove it by starting to pack," he says, smacking Andy on the back a little harder than is expressly necessary. He stands. "And then keep proving it by not flunking out. Though, then again, that probably would piss your mom off real good . . ."

"Dad."

Dad laughs. "I know, I know. I'm kidding," he says. "Partially."

Andy smiles and exhales as Dad kisses him on the forehead. And as the old man turns to leave the kitchen, Andy calls out again. "Hey, Dad?"

"Hmm?"

"What do I do about Shelbi?"

Dad looks over Andy's face. "You love her?" he asks.

Andy nods. "I really do, Dad."

"Well, it's an action verb. Which I'm *sure* you know, considering that perfect SAT verbal score." Dad makes his eyebrows bounce.

Andy just shakes his head. "You're *such* a parent."

"I'm *your* parent. Anyway, you gotta let her go."

Of course, Andy wants to resist this. He wants to resist it with everything he's got. Don't all the guys in the movies chase the woman down and declare their love over and over until they win her back?

Deep down, though, he knows Dad is right.

"Real love wants the best for the other person, even if isn't you," Dad continues. "If there's something you feel you need to say to her, do so in a way that doesn't violate any boundaries she's put in place. Then let her be. There's this old saying that I'm sure *you'll* think is 'whacked' or whatever, but trust me when I tell you it's true: If you love something, let it go. If it comes back, it's yours. If it doesn't, it wasn't."

Andy sighs. He hates getting hit with the dad-isms. Especially when they're so spot-on. "Yeah," he says. "Okay."

"Things'll work out how they need to, son. For both of us." Dad pats Andy's cheek and then makes his way out of the room.

Andy sinks down into the couch and stares out the window.

It's dusk.

He sighs. Sure hopes the old man is right.

PHASE 0.0

Stellar Debris

Love.

Shelbi really needed this workout.

She hasn't come to Arabia Mountain in over a month. Last time she made the hike, Walter was with her, and she's been afraid of what she might feel.

Today, though, she had to do it. He left for college three days ago, and this morning, Shelbi woke up feeling like it's high time she reclaims the spaces that were *hers* before he came into the picture.

She reaches her favorite little alcove at the top and unrolls her yoga mat.

As she raises her arms into the air to begin stretching, she keeps her eyes open because she knows if she closes them, Walter's face is all she'll see.

Deep breath.

Shelbi is a solid fifteen minutes into her piloga routine when she sees the envelope. It's held in place with a decent-size rock that isn't typically there, and based on how dingy and worn it looks, it's been there for at least a few days. (Thank goodness it hasn't rained in two weeks.)

At first, she just holds her plank pose, staring. Feeling all the stuff she's been trying to ignore well up inside her like the burning sensation in her stomach muscles.

She shifts to her knees and stares some more.

Has Shelbi been terrified that Walter thinks she hates him? Absolutely.

Does she hate him? Absolutely not.

In fact, looking at that envelope—which she is 110 percent sure is a letter to her from him—Shelbi can no longer deny that she *really* loves him.

But all of this is far more complex than she's ready to deal with. Especially right now. There are too many things happening at once. Like the fact that she starts her first semester of classes in five days. And is still going to therapy twice per week.

She takes a "prada-vaka" breath, as Becky puts it, then lifts the rock to remove the envelope from beneath it. Shelbi Camille, it says on the front in Walter's familiar scrawl. And before she loses her nerve, she removes the sheet of notebook paper inside, unfolds it, and begins to read.

Dear Shelbi,

Full disclosure: despite my SAT verbal score I'm not great at writing letters (this is my attempt at humor, please laugh). No idea how to even start this one, so I'm going to tell you about a conversation I had with my dad.

Actually wait. Before I do that, I need to tell you something else that you may already know? But I'll tell you anyway: my mom left. She's been cheating on

my dad for months with the one human on earth I
hate more than I hate going to the dentist. And she's
divorcing my dad. Additionally, she decided to move
out before I left for her alma mater.

So okay, groundwork laid.

The day Mom moved out, I wound up having this
supremely masculine heart-to-heart with my dad
(at one point we were both crying like giant man-
babies). And, surprise, surprise, you came up in the
conversation.

Let me first say: there's nothing in my life I
regret more than picking up a bottle the day that
I hurt you. And I'm very, very sorry, Shelbi. Yes, a
terrible thing had happened (literally CAUGHT my
mom cheating), but still. Going to Al-Anon meetings
with your mom (is that really bizarre for you?) has
really given me a lot of insight into how drinking can
damage both my relationships and the people I have
those relationships with.

It's weird writing about this.

All that said, I did want to tell you that I
have openly admitted to being an alcoholic, and I've
committed myself to sobriety. (Again, weird to write.)
I located both AA and Al-Anon chapters in Providence,
and I'll be going at least twice a week.

In addition to that wildly insufficient apology, I
also want to thank you. For the best summer of my
life. From Soup-Kitchen Saturdays and Piloga Tuesdays

to Stone Mountain Hike Thursdays and Superhero-Movie Fridays. From that first time we hugged to how I made a royal fool of myself when I met your parents. And from that amazing trip to the beach to me throwing you into your pool. From you rescuing me from Marcus's house to whooping me in Mortal Kombat. And then of course the highest highlight: our first kiss and us admitting we'd both broken the contract.

You've really been a gift to me, Shelbi. If you hadn't come up to me that Monday after my accident, given me my wallet, and made me feel less alone in the world, I genuinely don't know where I would be. (likely NOT headed to college, I'm sure.)

I know our paths are technically about to diverge or whatever, but I wanted you to know that I really do love you—even though I feel incredibly wack for saying it after my epic failure to show you it's true.

You're not speaking to me right now—and for good reason—and it would 100% be within your rights to never forgive me . . .

But I do hope you never forget how incredible you are. How kind and compassionate and loving and considerate. How giving and aware and illuminating.

You are, truly, the best thing to ever happen to me. And I know this will be the case for any human being lucky enough to get to call you a friend. I wish you the absolute best, Shelbi. And please know that if you ever need someone to talk to, I'm just a phone call away.

Okay, that's all I can think to say, so I'll stop now. OH, also please don't be mad at me for going to your Rendezvous Point with the Universe on my own. I promise I wasn't trying to be disrespectful or invasive . . . just needed to put this letter somewhere only you would find it. I really appreciate you sharing the location with me in the first place. Means a lot that you invited me into a space that's so special to you.

Love to you always. (MAN, I sound like such a cheeseball!)

Sincerely,
Walty Wal-Wal

Shelbi reads it twice.

And again.

So much has happened in such a short period of time. And so much more is coming.

She folds the letter and returns it to the envelope. Draws her knees up to her chest, stares out at the summer sky full of fluffy clouds, and allows herself to do the one thing she hasn't when it comes to Walter Andrew Criddle: feel and cry.

Over the good times. The conversations. The laughs. The gentle touches that made her shivery. The sweet, soft moments that reminded her she's alive—living, breathing, and feeling. And very much not alone.

She looks at the rock that was holding the envelope down. A rock Walter held in his hand and put into place. Because he was here. He came here. For her.

Because he didn't want her to be alone.

Shelbi has no idea how long she sits silently sobbing, but the next time she looks up, the sky has cleared and she's staring out at the most brilliant of blues.

She sighs. And smiles.

Shelbi Camille Augustine is not okay. (Which is perfectly okay.)

She *is* deeply in love with Walter Andrew Criddle, though. There's no doubt about that.

She's just not ready. At all. She knows that as saliently as she knows how nervous she is about this totally uncharted next phase of life she's about to step into.

She's not ready for the butterflies or skipped heartbeats. For the sweaty palms or irresistible smiles. She's not ready for the warm feeling in her chest when their thoughts and feelings align, or for the inevitable disagreements because they are two different people who have been shaped by different experiences.

Shelbi isn't ready. Not even close.

But it's fine. Because she knows: eventually . . .

she will be.

Author's Note

Well, hello again!

First, thank you for reading this book all the way to the end (almost *smirks*). It's wonderful to know that the writing was not in vain. For those of you living with any form of neurotransmittal atypicality (yes, I did create that term), know that you are heroes to me. As hard as it is at times, try to remember this: each of us has been making an impact on the world since conception. I mean that. The moment the individuals who birthed us realized we were inside their wombs, *everything* changed for them. Which means it also shifted for the people around those individuals. And the people around those people. And on and on and on like the ripples from a pebble tossed into a still lake.

Another fact: every room you step into shifts the moment you enter it. I believe that whether it shifts positively or negatively is wholly up to you. You get to decide what you bring into the spaces where you set your feet.

To *all* readers, I have one last favor to ask: wherever you are, please take a moment to read the following words aloud (whisper if you must):

MENTAL HEALTH IS JUST AS IMPORTANT AS
PHYSICAL HEALTH.

So much so, the two are inextricably linked.

I ask you to read it aloud because there's power in hearing it, even from your own lips. Shelbi and Walter are fictional characters, but their respective maladies— bipolar disorder and alcoholism (which is classified as a Substance Abuse Disorder in the *Diagnostic and Statistical Manual of Mental Disorders*)—are as real as the oxygen flowing into your lungs to keep you alive right now. And in order to stay *physically* healthy, they both have to be *mentally* healthy.

Chaos Theory was born out of a deep frustration with the stigma attached to mental illness. I wasn't diagnosed until I was in my thirties, but at twenty-one, one of my best friends was diagnosed with a major depressive disorder. In scientific terms, there was an issue with the way her brain was handling serotonin, one of the brain chemicals that regulate mood, so a psychiatrist prescribed a selective serotonin reuptake inhibitor (SSRI) antidepressant to help regulate her serotonin functioning and pull her out of the abyss, so to speak.

I will never forget (or cease to be bothered by) the shame I heard in her voice when she called and told me, "The shrink put me on pills." Because of mental illness stigma, she was embarrassed that she needed medication for a disease she couldn't "see."

Fact: the human brain is an organ that is just as susceptible to damage and dysfunction as any other organ. Because the brain is our center of reason and selfhood, said fact is unnerving . . . but that doesn't make it any less true. Cognitive functioning is based on delicate balances of hormones, neurotransmitters—the naturally occurring chemicals in the brain that control our moods—and electrochemical signals. So needing assistance from medication to maintain these balances is no different from needing an insulin pump to do what a dysfunctional pancreas can't do.

My point in all this: being diagnosed with a mental disorder—be it bipolar disorder, BDD (with anorexia, bulimia, or the like), OCD, ADD/ADHD, GAD, panic disorder, schizophrenia/schizoaffective disorder, SAD, MDD, trichotillomania, PTSD, DID/MPD, etc., etc.—does *not* decrease an individual's inherent worth. We are not scourges or mistakes or menaces to society or freaks of nature or freaks in general. We are not "faking it." We cannot just buck up, man up, perk up, or get up. And we are not bringing it on ourselves or "being psycho for no reason" or "trying to get attention."

Frailty comes in all shapes, sizes, colors, and disorders: asthma, achy joints, heart disease, migraines, dislocated elbows, cancer, generalized anxiety disorder, schizophrenia . . .

Their commonality? Human beings.

Also, I lied before. I have one more favor to ask. Well . . . Shelbi does:

Please read the following agreement carefully, and if you're willing to abide by the terms, add your signature on the line provided.

Mental Health Advocate (MHA) Agreement

1. I will do my best not to use any mental illness slurs, including but not limited to: crazy, psycho, lunatic, nutjob, cuckoo, wacko, spaz, crackpot, head case, and any and all derivatives, noun, adjective, or otherwise.

2. I will respect the fact that individuals living with any and all forms of mental illness are valuable just the way they are, and will seek to understand them instead of making unfair judgments.

3. I will not make fun of mental illness, and I will avoid using mental illness terminology flippantly (like saying someone is "bipolar" because I don't like how they're acting or saying someone is "psychotic" because I don't understand why they do the things they do).

4. I will acknowledge the seriousness of mental disorders and not accuse people of "faking it."

5. If someone I know is diagnosed with a mental disorder, I won't be a jerk about it. I am not required to join their support team, but I will exercise empathy to the best of my ability.

6. I will not, under any circumstances, cease to treat individuals living with mental disorders as human

beings who are valuable additions to the world at large.

X: _____

Date: _____

Awesome.
Now turn the page. ☺

EPILOGUE

Stellar Nebula 2.0

Hello?

Walter?

Is this still your number?

Uhhh . . .

Sorry.

I think you have the wrong person.

Oh my gosh! I'm so sorry!

What you ARE is adorably gullible.

It's been three months, Shelbi. Not three years.

Of course this is still my number.

You seriously get on my nerves.

But also, fair point.

Hahahahaha!

Damn, I've missed you.

Cut it out.

I'm serious!

Wouldn't be a stretch to say I've been praying this day would come for . . . a while.

Oh hush.

I can imagine your face right now and the cuteness is killing me.

So how you been, Queen?

"Queen" huh?

Absolutely.

The Black Student Union up here has IMPACTED your boy.

Lol this is amazing.

I've been good!

I mean . . . as evidenced by the fact that I reached out to you.

Valid. Lol.

So how have YOU been?

Sober. ☺

That's so good to hear, Wal.

Oh no, you called me Wal.

I don't know if you can do that, Shelbi.

It does things to me.

Hahahaha! My bad.

Pfffft.

You are 100% not sorry.

Lol.

So, how's school? You haven't flunked out, have you? My dad would be pretty disappointed . . .

I had lunch with your dad yesterday, in fact.

I want to start a weekend program for kids at the planetarium, and he's going to help me pull it all together.

For YOUR sake, I will pretend not to be jealous that the old man got to bask in your presence while I'm up here freezing my ass off in Rhode Island.

Yeah I don't even know how you're doing that.

Shelbi plus snow equals big no-go.

Man.

I would really love to see and hear you say that aloud.

My poetic prowess is staggering, isn't it?

Anyway, to answer your question, school is good.

It's actually the reason I reached out. I learned something in one of my classes a couple days ago that . . . helped me see some things a little differently, I guess.

And I've been thinking about it a lot.

Aw snap, Shelbi Camille Augustine is about to nerd out.

My fingertips are literally tingling right now.

I seriously can't stand you sometimes . . .

Hahahaha!

(Totally walked out of class to talk to you, by the way.)

(You're welcome.)

I would scold you, but I know it's futile.

Anyway, there's this thing called chaos theory.

Granted: I don't FULLY understand it and
I have quite a bit of studying to do before
this exam next Wednesday . . .

But the gist is there are systems governed
by hard and fast deterministic laws
that exhibit apparently random and/or
unpredictable behaviors.

You're 100% speaking science geek right
now, but I can assure you I am rapt.

I'll give you an example: you've seen
a pinball machine before, yeah?

That I have.

Okay so if you think about the way those are
designed, there's a slight incline to them . . .

And the goal is to keep the ball from rolling
all the way down to the bottom.

Yep. I follow.

Well, the physics of the game are simple. Whole thing is based on gravity.

But still: it would be difficult to predetermine the trajectory of the ball because it's based on a bunch of tiny variables like angles and the amount of force with which the ball is initially hit.

Understood.

So in a nutshell, things are only "unpredictable" because it's impossible to know all the variables.

Makes sense.

Which got me to thinking . . .

Oh boy . . . that's never good . . .

Oh shut up.

My point: it hit me that if it's impossible to know all the variables involved in something as concrete as a ball traveling down a decline . . . how much MORE impossible must it be to know all the variables involved in any given interaction between highly complex human beings?

An excellent application of some obscure science thing to real life, Dr. Augustine.

Umm . . . Dr. Augustine is my father.

I . . .

Wow that was perfect.

You're welcome.

As I was saying: this whole thing shifted my perspective on some things pretty saliently.

This chaos theory thing you mean.

(Also you are SUPER in nerd-mode using words like "saliently." It's doing things to me the same way "Wal" does.)

Yes. The chaos theory thing.

(Ignoring your other comment.)

And what is this salient shift you've experienced, m'lady?

Basically: trying to predict what will happen at any given moment between two vastly complex human beings is futile.

There are too many variables.

That makes far more sense than I'm expressly comfortable with. Lol.

Right. Because we like to think we're in control of things.

You can certainly say that again.

Walter, I am still very much in love with you.

Probably even more so than the last time we spoke.

Uhh . . .

Wow.

Sheesh, Shelbi.

Can a guy get a warning next time you decide to flip it on him??

I'm serious.

I read (present tense) that letter you left me literally every day.

I love you more than I've ever loved anyone.

Well . . . outside of my parents and Becky.

Hahahaha!

Man, I've missed you so much.

I've missed you too, Wal-Wal.

Definitely NOT going back to class because I'm probably gonna go cry when this conversation is over.

Cry??

Shelbi, literally every single bit of me wanting to be a better dude and keep my stuff together has to do with you.

And my therapist here (I have one!) has helped me get okay with that.

Oh.

I see.

In other words: I love you too, Shelbi.

Face is warm now, thanks.

Welcome to the party.

At least your skin is brown enough for it to not show.

Soooooo . . .

When will you be home?

Well let's get right to it then!

Shut up.

Nope.

Couple weeks. Friday before
Thanksgiving week.

Do you want to umm . . .
go on a date with me?

Hold on, gimme a sec.

Need to give myself a good pinch
to make sure I'm not dreaming.

Did the most beautiful girl in the universe
just ask me on a date?

Oh my god, just answer!

Okay, okay, my bad!

Yes, Shelbi. I would love to go
on a date with you.

Okay good.

I'll pick you up at 7 on the Friday you get here?

Let's make it 5.

I get in at 3, and have zero doubt the extra couple of hours would murder me.

Lol.

So dramatic.

It's a date then.

Oh man. What am I gonna WEAR??

You're ridiculous.

Also: you really should go back to class.

HA!

You think I could focus in class knowing my future girlfriend is one of the first faces I'll see when I come home?

Whoa now. Cool it with the whole "girlfriend" thing.

Baby steps, Wal-Wal.

Hahahahaha!

I knew you were gonna say that.

So I'll see you soon?

Nowhere near soon enough. But yes.

Okay. Have a great rest of your day, Walter!

Oh, you bet your cute butt I will.

Excuse you, don't be looking at my butt.

Ehhhh . . . too late?

Man, you are the worst.

And I adore you.

Totally mutual, my love.

Now I have to go to class.
And unlike you, I'm not skipping.

Suit yourself, Nerd Girl.

Kiss kiss!

If I'm a nerd, you're a dork.

Yup. A dork for you.

That was galactically corny.

And doesn't even make sense.

Sometimes love is illogical, girl.

WOW that sounded like a Marcus Page line.

Gross.

Lol, you're not wrong, and it was pretty terrible.

Now go ahead and get to what is surely some advanced astrochemical microbiology class.

You're . . . not actually that far off.

It's Gravitational Wave Astrophysics.

Of course it is, you supergenius.

13 days.

I can hardly wait.

Acknowledgments

That time again: Nic sits down to write acknowledgments and blanks on who all she needs to thank. Also, this book is being published during a time when a global pandemic keeps reinventing itself like a former child star, and there are paper shortages and stuff as a result, so I don't actually have a ton of space to get all woo-woo anyway. So I will make it fast and very few actual names will be mentioned. . . .

Because, frankly, there were SO many people across literal years of time—eight and a half years elapsed between when I initially wrote this book and when it published—who helped me make this book what it is. From an agent who saw potential in it to the point of offering representation, to early beta readers (y'all remember when Shelbi's chapters were written as letters to God?), to authenticity readers (definitely had a problematic trope here or there initially), to mental health professionals, to an editor who let me pull it back out of the desk drawer and dust it off . . . then helped me cut it in half.

And I'm also thankful for you, dear reader. If you're *still* reading, you clearly care.

I am eternally grateful.